Praise for Marta Perry

"Marta Perry writes very sensitive and generous characters that many will relate to."
—*RT Book Reviews*

"This first in Perry's mini-series about the Bodines gets off to a fine start with charming characters and the struggle to understand loss and move on."
—*RT Book Reviews* on *Twice in a Lifetime*

"*Mission: Motherhood* is a terrific family story. Kudos to Marta Perry for such an inspiring novel."
—*RT Book Reviews*

"A wonderful story about renewing your faith after failures and the twists life can take. *Final Justice* will please readers looking for a message within the story."
—*Romance Readers Connection*

Praise for Betsy St. Amant

"St. Amant pens an entertaining story."
—*RT Book Reviews* on *Rodeo Sweetheart*

"A lovely story about old friends who discover that, with God's help, the good things from the past can be appreciated and carried into a new future."
—*RT Book Reviews* on *Return to Love*

"Betsy St. Amant tells a great story and her characters are so real. I enjoyed every minute of it and highly recommend it to anyone."
—Sarah Varland, The Lamb's Well Christian Bookstore, on *Return to Love*

MARTA PERRY

has written everything from Sunday school curricula to travel articles to magazine stories in more than twenty years of writing, but she feels she's found her writing home in the stories she writes for the Love Inspired lines.

Marta lives in rural Pennsylvania, but she and her husband spend part of each year at their second home in South Carolina. When she's not writing, she's probably visiting her children and her six beautiful grandchildren, traveling, gardening or relaxing with a good book.

Marta loves hearing from readers, and she'll write back with a signed bookmark and/or her brochure of Pennsylvania Dutch recipes. Write to her c/o Steeple Hill Books, 233 Broadway, Suite 1001, New York, NY 10279, e-mail her at marta@martaperry.com or visit her on the Web at www.martaperry.com.

BETSY ST. AMANT

loves polka-dot shoes, chocolate and sharing the good news of God's grace through her novels. She has a bachelor's degree in Christian communications from Louisiana Baptist University and is actively pursuing a career in inspirational writing. Betsy resides in northern Louisiana with her husband and daughter and enjoys reading, kickboxing and spending quality time with her family.

MISTLETOE PRAYERS

MARTA PERRY
BETSY ST. AMANT

Steeple Hill®

Published by Steeple Hill Books™

STEEPLE HILL BOOKS

Steeple Hill®

PLEASE RECYCLE · THIS PRODUCT IS RECYCLABLE

Recycling programs for this product may not exist in your area.

ISBN-13: 978-0-373-81505-0

MISTLETOE PRAYERS

Copyright © 2010 by Harlequin Books S.A.

The publisher acknowledges the copyright holders of the individual works as follows:

THE BODINE FAMILY CHRISTMAS
Copyright © 2010 by Martha Johnson

THE GINGERBREAD SEASON
Copyright © 2010 by Betsy St. Amant

This edition published by arrangement with Steeple Hill Books.

® and TM are trademarks of Steeple Hill Books, used under license. Trademarks indicated with ® are registered in the United States Patent and Trademark Office, the Canadian Trade Marks Office and in other countries.

www.SteepleHill.com

Printed in U.S.A.

CONTENTS

THE BODINE
FAMILY CHRISTMAS

Marta Perry

THE BODINE
FAMILY CHRISTMAS

Marta Perry

This story is dedicated to the memory of my dear
sister-in-law, Patricia Nelson. And, as always,
to Brian, with much love.

How great is the love the Father has lavished on us,
that we should be called children of God!
—1 *John* 3:1

Chapter One

Lieutenant Travis McCall had never had what most people would call a merry Christmas, and it was the last thing he wanted this year. The glossy door of the Southern colonial house bore a huge Christmas wreath, and the sight was nearly enough to make him turn tail.

Almost, but not quite. He'd promised his buddy, and he never went back on his word.

The moment's hesitation proved just enough. A discordant bray pierced the air of Mt. Pleasant, the quiet Charleston suburb. He glanced toward the driveway, which swept around the house, and blinked. A horse trailer had been pulled there, its ramp down. On the ramp, all four feet planted firmly, stood a small gray donkey.

A lead rope disappeared into the back of the trailer. Someone out of Travis's sight in the trailer was apparently trying to pull the donkey in. Just as plainly, the donkey didn't intend to go anywhere. Travis had loaded horses and cattle enough times as a kid to know the signs.

Even as he thought it, the animal jerked back. In a minute it would be free, running into traffic as likely as not. He'd have to go give that idiot a hand.

A few quick strides took him across the lawn. Just as he reached the ramp, the donkey reared, yanking the lead rope. A slight figure hurtled out of the back of the trailer, stumbled on the ramp and barreled into Travis.

He grasped it, his mind registering several things at once. This was not a teenage boy, as his first startled glimpse had made him think. And the donkey, managing to free himself, bolted.

"Are you okay?" He grasped the woman under the elbows, setting her on her feet.

"Never mind me. Help me get that foolish beast before he gets himself hit by a car." Even the sharpness of the command couldn't deprive the woman's voice of a soft Southern drawl, reminding him of Luke Bodine.

He let go of her. "I'll get between him and the street."

"Good. Don't scare him." Deep blue eyes were focused on the donkey, not sparing a glance for him.

"I'm not the one who lost him," he reminded her. The donkey had dropped his head to crop at the grass. Travis moved a few steps to the side, to be in a position to intercept him if he should take a notion to head for the street.

The woman grinned, not taking offense at his words. "True enough. I thought the hay in the rack would be enough to tempt him in. Guess I was wrong." She pulled a carrot from the pocket of her denim jacket. "Maybe this will do it."

This obviously had to be Annabel Bodine, Travis decided, watching as she crooned to the donkey, coaxing him with the carrot. Luke often talked about his twin sisters. Amanda was a reporter while Annabel ran some kind of animal shelter.

Annabel, with her faded jeans, scuffed boots and denim jacket, fit the part. Long blond hair was pulled back into a single heavy braid, and her heart-shaped face was innocent of makeup. The smattering of freckles on her cheeks made her look like a kid.

"There, now, you silly boy. Nobody's going to hurt you ever again."

The donkey's white muzzle extended toward the treat, and he sniffed cautiously.

If it were up to Travis, he'd have made a grab for the rope already, but he had to admit Annabel seemed to know what she was doing. She continued to talk softly to the donkey as he chomped at the carrot, running her hand down his neck and finally taking hold of the rope.

"There, now. That wasn't so bad, was it?" She led him toward the trailer.

Travis moved in behind, ready to jump into action if the animal showed signs of trouble, but the donkey—apparently having decided this woman was a friend—moved into the trailer and began to eat hay as if that had always been his plan.

Annabel slipped out the side door of the trailer. Together, they shut the tailgate.

"Sorry." She looked up at him with a quicksilver smile that reminded him of his friend. "That wasn't exactly the welcome we had planned for you. You must be Travis McCall. I'm Annabel Bodine, Luke's sister."

She extended her hand, seemed to remember the donkey had been eating the carrot from it and wiped it on her jeans instead.

"I figured that. Luke said you worked with animals." He glanced at the donkey as he spoke, and his eyes narrowed. "That animal has been abused."

"Yes." Sorrow deepened the blue of Annabel's eyes. "That's why he's going home with me. It won't ever happen again."

He nodded. In his book, there wasn't much worse than a man who'd abuse a helpless animal—unless it was a man who'd do that to a child. He shut that thought away with a forcible slam.

Annabel brushed some gray fur from the sleeve

of his dress blues. "Sorry again. But you didn't need to get all dressed up to come see us, you know."

"If I'm calling on a superior officer, I dress accordingly," he said. The Bodines were a military family. Luke's father was a senior officer at the U.S. Coast Guard Base in Charleston, South Carolina, where Travis had just been posted, coming from the base in Kodiak, Alaska, where he'd met Luke Bodine.

Annabel took his arm, her hand small and capable. "Come on, then. Let's get you introduced to Mamma and Daddy. They'll be thrilled you're here. And I warn you, they'll want to know every little bitty thing about what Luke's been up to since he left here."

She led him across the veranda and threw open the door, tugging him into a wide center hall. Could she sense his nervousness? If so, she seemed determined not to let him give in to it.

"Mamma! Daddy! He's here!" She brushed the long braid of honey-blond hair back over the shoulder of her denim jacket.

She glanced up at him, and again he noticed the spray of freckles across her cheeks. Luke had called her his tomboy kid sister. She was that, but there was a grown-up appeal in her wide blue eyes and generous mouth.

He jerked his mind away from those thoughts. This was his buddy's sister. And those were his parents, hurrying toward them from somewhere in the rear of the house.

He might prefer to spend his Christmas alone in his quarters, safe from people pitying him, but there was no getting away from it now. Like it or not, he'd be having this Christmas with the Bodine family.

Annabel didn't miss the stiffening of Travis's already erect military bearing as her parents approached from the family room at the back of the house. Was he that much in awe of a superior officer?

Daddy was just…well, Daddy. Still, he did have a quick temper, paired with an expectation that anybody around him would always do his or her best. She could see the brand-new Coasties being a bit afraid. But Travis was an officer, a helicopter pilot and a good friend of Luke's to boot.

Having him here for Christmas wouldn't be like having her brother home. That thought lay behind the introductions she performed. She allowed herself a wistful look back at last Christmas, when Luke had kept her too busy to think about her own problems. About the fiancé who'd dumped her and the Christmas wedding that hadn't happened.

Travis seemed to thaw as Mamma chattered away to him in that soft Southern voice of hers. Annabel watched, keeping a determined smile on her face. Anybody would think her pain and humiliation would have disappeared by now, but she could still feel it, nibbling at her heart as the holiday approached. Well, she wouldn't let it in.

"Sugar, what are you frownin' about?" Mamma turned to her with one of her quick movements. "Is that donkey stowed away where he can't get into any trouble?"

"Yes, ma'am, he's in the trailer, eatin' his way through the hay. I reckon he'll be all right until I get him to the farm."

"Not that I mind finding an abandoned donkey in the back garden when I get up in the morning," Daddy said, his humor hiding behind the mock glare he directed at her. "But he was chowing down on the wisteria we put in last spring."

"Good thing it wasn't the holly," she said, "or we'd have one sick donkey on our hands."

"We wouldn't want that," Daddy said, the smile reaching his voice. "But really, sugar, if folks are going to start dumping their strays here instead of out at the farm—"

"Now, Daddy, you know that's the first time it ever happened, and I'm sure it will be the last." She hoped. "You ought to see what shows up at the farm sometimes."

Travis was looking a little bewildered.

"The farm I own is an animal refuge," she explained. "The humane society can manage the dogs and cats that people dump off, but they really don't have the facilities for anything any bigger. So those animals come to my farm."

He nodded. "Luke did mention something about that when he was telling me about you."

She couldn't help wincing, hoping that her big brother hadn't seen fit to tell his friend all about her. "I can imagine what he said. 'It's easy to tell the twins apart, because Annabel's the tomboy.'"

"That's just about it." Travis smiled, the somewhat stern cast of his face relaxing with the words, sun lines crinkling around his chocolate-brown eyes, and her heart gave an unexpected little thump.

"We want to hear every single thing about Luke," Mamma interrupted. "But sugar, if you're going to get that donkey settled at the farm and make yourself presentable for supper, hadn't you best get moving?"

She glanced at her watch. "I will, Mamma. Don't worry. Sam will help with the donkey, and I'll be back in plenty of time for supper." Since her teenage helper lived at the farm, he could take over.

"Dress up a little, sugar." Mamma patted her cheek gently. "It is a party, after all." She glanced at Travis. "Nothing too elaborate, mind. Just some of the family coming over for supper and to help us trim the tree. To welcome you to Charleston."

A wave of sympathy swept through Annabel when she saw Travis's expression. If he was this shaken by meeting Mamma and Daddy, he'd be downright flattened when he encountered a whole big mess of Bodines, all overflowing with eagerness to welcome him to an old-fashioned low-country Christmas.

"No, thanks." Annabel disentangled the tinsel her twin, Amanda, was trying to wrap around Annabel's braid. "I don't care to look like a Christmas tree."

"Come on, sugar." Amanda put a silver bell on the tree and considered the effect. "I was just trying to make you look a little more festive for our guest. We want to make this a good Christmas for him, don't we?"

Recognizing her twin's matchmaking talent coming to the fore, Annabel forced herself not to react. That would only encourage her. Amanda and Mamma had spent much of the past two years introducing her to a parade of eligible men, aided and abetted by every other member of the Bodine clan.

Only her grandmother, Miz Callie, seemed to understand that Annabel wasn't ready to risk her heart again. Maybe she never would be.

"I'm sure everyone is making Travis feel welcome," she said. "You ought to be worried about your own beau, shouldn't you? Ross and Daddy are over in the corner, and the chances they're agreeing on anything are pretty slim, don't you think?"

"Goodness, I'd best get over there before they start arguing about politics." Amanda shoved a Christmas ornament into Annabel's hand and darted off toward the two most important men in her life.

Annabel had been fairly sure that would divert her twin. Since Amanda had fallen in love with Ross when he'd been investigating Daddy in his role as newspaper editor, it wasn't surprising that Ross and Daddy acted like two dogs with one bone over Amanda from time to time.

She shifted her gaze to Travis. He was talking to Hugh, her other brother, probably about Luke. Travis had been putting on a good front, but she could see that he wasn't entirely comfortable with the festivities. At least Mamma had had sense enough not to invite the whole clan. Still, just her siblings, Miz Callie, Great-Uncle Ned and a couple of cousins made an intimidating enough bunch.

"Are you trimming or daydreaming?" Her cousin Georgia's voice held laughter. "You've been holding that same ornament for ages."

"I was just waiting for Lindsay." She smiled at Georgia's eight-year-old. "It's so pretty with the stars on it that I thought she'd like to put it on the tree."

Lindsay took the ball carefully in two hands. "Can I really, Mamma? It's beautiful."

"You surely can, sugar." Georgia's face lit with the pleasure she always showed when her stepdaughter called her Mamma.

As they decided on the proper place for the special ornament, Annabel glanced toward Travis again. Her fingers clenched. Hugh had brought over the stepladder, and he seemed to be expecting Travis to climb up it to hang the kissing ball from the chandelier.

Didn't he remember that Travis was just off the sick list? She moved toward them quickly as Travis put one foot on the ladder.

"What are you doing, Hugh? Trying to foist your job off on someone else?"

"He wants to, Bel. Honest." Hugh, laughing, held his hands up as if to defend himself against an attack.

She touched Travis's arm, to find it resembled nothing so much as a steel bar. "You don't have to climb—"

"I'm cleared for duty." The snap in his voice told her that was a sensitive point.

"Sorry," she said softly. She started to turn away, but his warm clasp on her hand brought her gaze back to his face.

"No, I'm the one who's sorry. Guess I hate being reminded."

His fingers lingered on hers a moment longer, and her heart gave a silly little thump that startled and dismayed her. She couldn't…she didn't want…

She took a firm hold of herself and managed a smile. "Well, the truth is that Hugh shouldn't go scampering around on ladders anyway."

Hugh tugged her braid in retribution. "I'm fine, half-pint."

"That's men for you." Miz Callie, her grandmother, entered the fray. "Always think they can't admit being less than strong, but let them get sick, and they act like babies. Now, you two big strong men hold that wobbly stepladder and let Annabel put up the kissing ball. It's her turn anyway."

"Right." She scampered up before they could argue, reaching down for the mistletoe-and-holly confection and hooking it into place. "Does that look right?"

"Looks fine to me," Miz Callie said. "Come down quick before Amanda wants to argue about whose turn it is." She turned to Travis. "Have you figured out the difference between the twins yet?"

"I had a head start, ma'am. Luke told me what to look for."

Annabel hopped down to the floor. "He said Amanda was the sophisticated one and I was the tomboy."

Travis's gaze rested on her face in a way she found disconcerting. "Not quite. He said Amanda glittered but you glow. I think he was right."

Her cheeks flushed, but she was spared trying to think of an answer by Miz Callie's quick hug.

"I declare, I think that boy must be growing up if he said that." Miz Callie released her, turning her bright, birdlike glance on Travis. "You and my grandson are good friends. It gives us a lot of pleasure to welcome you here."

"Thank you, ma'am. It's kind of you to offer me your hospitality." Travis's deep voice was respectful. He might not exude the Southern charm the Bodine men had in abundance, but he knew how to treat a lady.

"You make sure you come out to the beach house to see me, y'heah? My grandchildren's friends are always welcome in my home."

Miz Callie's warmth embraced Travis as a matter of course. She didn't know, because Luke had told only Annabel, the deeper reasons why Luke was so insistent on their giving his friend a real Christmas.

It was the helicopter crash in which Travis had put himself in peril in order to see his crew to safety. It was the woman he'd loved, who apparently hadn't cared enough to wait out his recuperation.

Make sure Travis has a good Christmas. Her brother's voice echoed in her mind. *I'm counting on you, Annabel.*

She'd promised, her heart touched. But that was before she'd met Travis, before she'd felt that warning signal that her own heart might be in danger if she got too close.

Mamma brought in cookies and hot chocolate, diverting the attention of everyone but the children, who were too excited about the tree to stop, even for cookies.

Annabel took her cup and retired to the rocker

in the corner, wrestling with the problem that had dropped so unexpectedly into her lap. She couldn't let Luke down, but…

Surely it would be enough if she saw to it that Travis was kept occupied. After all, the whole family wanted to get in on the act. It didn't have to involve her so much, did it?

"…and then there's the Jaycees' Christmas dance, and the hospital auxiliary party, and the boat parade and…" Mamma's voice floated over the chatter as she outlined the plans she'd made for Travis's entertainment over the holidays.

And Travis, well, Travis looked as if he'd like to jump on the first plane back to Alaska.

"Goodness, Julia, let the boy breathe, won't you?" Great-Uncle Ned came, surprisingly, to Travis's rescue. "He doesn't look to me as if he's one for the social whirl, are you, son?"

"Not exactly. I mean, I'm grateful, but…" He stumbled to a halt, probably afraid he'd offend someone no matter what he said.

"I know just what you'd like," Miz Callie said, reaching across the sofa to pat his arm. "You ought to go out to the farm and help Annabel with the animals. Goodness knows she could always use an extra pair of hands, especially with getting all the creatures ready for the Living Nativity. Luke said you grew up on a ranch, so that ought to be just the thing for you. How does that sound?"

Annabel couldn't miss the relief in his eyes. "I'd be happy to help out, if Annabel could use me."

He looked at her. Everyone looked at her. It was obvious what she had to say, so she said it.

"I'd love to have your help, Travis. Thank you." And her hopes of keeping a safe distance from Travis McCall went fizzling away to nothing.

Chapter Two

Peaceable Farm. The white sign with blue lettering was nearly obscured by the vines that grew around it. Travis turned into the lane. Peaceable. A nice name, bringing with it visions of peace and tranquility.

Like Annabel. There was something still and serene in the depths of her blue eyes, reminding him of a quiet mountain lake he'd seen once.

She'd agreed quickly enough to her grandmother's suggestion that he help out, and he'd been so thankful to be rescued from Mrs. Bodine's social calendar that he hadn't stopped to consider anything else. Later, thinking it through, he'd begun to wonder.

Had there been some slight hesitation in her eyes before she spoke? If she really didn't want him here—well, he ought to be able to tell by her reactions to his presence. He could make some excuse to get out of this.

The gravel lane wound around a sprawling white

farmhouse and under the twisted branches of trees draped with Spanish moss. Even in December, flowers were blooming, and he spared a quick thought for the weather in Kodiak at the moment. No wonder Luke longed for home.

He was still smiling at the thought when he came out into the open behind the house and the farm spread out before him—a red barn, a paddock, several fenced pastures beyond. And Annabel, walking toward the car with what seemed a genuine expression of welcome.

He parked under a sprawling live oak and got out.

"You found us all right." Annabel, in well-worn jeans, scuffed boots and a flannel shirt worn loose over a T-shirt, didn't show any signs of wanting him gone. "These backroads can be tough for a stranger."

"Your father gave me good directions. All I had to do was keep my eyes open for your sign. I like the name. How did you come up with it?"

"Peaceable kingdom. You know...the image in the Bible of the future time when the lion shall lie down with the lamb."

"I see." He didn't, but he didn't want to admit it.

"Not that I have any lions," Annabel said. She started toward the barn, and he fell into step with her. "But there are lambs—well, sheep, anyway." She gestured toward the fenced pasture.

A few cows, several sheep, an annoyed-looking goat and what looked like… "Is that really a llama?"

She nodded. "It really is. Silly, isn't it? People think they want an unusual pet. Then, when they find out how much trouble the animals are, they want to throw them away, as if they were disposable toys instead of living creatures." The thread of anger in her voice showed him that on this one subject, at least, Annabel wasn't so serene.

"People do that." With kids, also, as he knew only too well.

She darted a look at his face. "Have you decided yet if I'm crazy?"

He grinned, shaking his head. "Not crazy. Just a little idealistic, maybe."

"That's what people say when…" She cut off the words when a kid came out of the barn—a gangly teenager in jeans and a shirt that had seen better days. "Everything okay, Sam?"

The boy shot an appraising, wary glance at Travis. "Sure thing. I got that donkey in the cross ties, but he's not likin' it very much."

"It's a first step, anyway. Travis, this is Sam Jefferson. He helps me out here. Sam, meet Travis McCall. He's the coast-guard friend of my brother's I was telling you about."

"Nice to meet you, Sam." Travis extended his hand.

The boy put his out reluctantly, it seemed, distrust in his dark eyes. "Yeah." He swung back to Annabel. "You want me to help out with the donkey?"

"I'll have Travis do that. You can go on back to the fencing you were working on this morning."

"If you say so." Face tight, he walked off.

"Sorry about that," Annabel said once the boy was out of earshot. "He's a little cautious with strangers."

"Seemed like he didn't want me doing his job. If my being here is going to cause problems…" He let his voice trail off, giving her the chance to find an out if she wanted one.

"No, not at all." She shook her head, the long braid swinging. "Sam…well, he comes from a difficult family situation. After Sam's mother died, he really needed a job and a place to stay. And I needed someone good with animals, so it all worked out."

"Good." The word sounded strangled, and he hoped she didn't notice. He understood about difficult family situations too well.

They moved through the open barn door, from sunlight into shadow. The donkey was the sole occupant, it seemed, except for a barn swallow that swooped out the door when they entered.

Secure in the cross ties that attached to his halter on either side, the donkey rolled his eyes as Annabel approached him.

"He doesn't look like he's feeling any too friendly," Travis pointed out. "What exactly are we going to do?"

"The vet left some ointment for his sores." Annabel bent to pick up a brush from a plastic caddy on the floor. "I'd like to get some of the burrs out of his coat and put the ointment on." She glanced at him. "Do you want to help? Because it's okay if you don't."

"Just tell me what you want me to do." He rolled back his sleeves as he spoke. That donkey wasn't as big as some animals he'd dealt with, but it could probably get in a wicked kick if anyone was foolish enough to be within range.

"Let me try to calm him first. Then you can hold his head and talk to him while I work on him. There now, Toby." She transferred her attention from him to the donkey. "Nobody's going to hurt you here. We're going to take care of you."

"He doesn't look convinced," Travis said. "If he was abandoned, how do you know his name is Toby?"

"I don't." She touched the animal's neck, and his ears went back. "It's a traditional name for a donkey, so that's what I called him." She began stroking the neck. "Keep talking. I think he likes the sound of our voices."

He thought she was overly optimistic, but he

obeyed. "Tell me about this Living Nativity your grandmother mentioned. I've never heard of that."

"You haven't?" Her hand moved gently, rhythmically. "Maybe it's not so popular in other places, but our church has had one every year since I can remember. We build a three-sided stable on the church lawn, and then the children and teenagers act out the Christmas story. And of course we use real animals."

Of course. "Camels?"

"Well, no, not camels." She sounded regretful, and he suspected if she could come up with a camel, there'd be one. "Cows, sheep, goats. Definitely a donkey for Mary to ride on."

"And you figure Toby is going to be ready for that?" At her gesture, he moved closer, taking her place at the animal's head as she began to brush.

"Well...let's just say I hope so." She moved the brush gently over the matted coat. "True, there's not a lot of time, but love and gentleness can rehabilitate any hurting creature, don't you think?"

What he thought was that she was naive and probably a little too trusting. Hurting creatures could turn on anyone, even a person as gentle as Annabel.

"How did you get involved with this, anyway?" He patted the donkey's muzzle, keeping his hands well away from its teeth.

"Miz Callie," she said promptly. She put down the brush and began applying ointment. "My grandmother never saw a hurting creature she didn't try to help. And the way she looks after the sea turtle nests out at the island—well, it's too bad you weren't here for the hatching. That's—"

He saw trouble coming too late to speak. The donkey's skin shivered, his rear end shifted and he kicked out. Annabel tumbled back, landing half on a bale of straw.

Abandoning the animal, he rushed to her. "Are you okay?"

"I'm fine." She pushed herself up. "I felt it coming and got out of the way of his hooves." She sat down suddenly on the straw bale, making him suspect she wasn't as calm about it as she'd let on.

"You sure?" He frowned down at her.

"Positive. Goodness, it's not the first time I've taken a tumble. You grew up on a ranch. You must be used to getting bumped around."

He was—but not by the animals. His face must have changed, because all at once she was looking at him with a question in those wide blue eyes.

"Sure thing." He held out his hand to her. What was he doing, letting this woman push him into giving himself away? "I'm just surprised. I always thought Southern women were fragile flowers."

A chuckle escaped her, and she clasped his hand and let him raise her to her feet. "Don't let any of the women in my family hear you say that. Steel magnolias, every one of them."

She looked into his face, her hand still clasped in his. The wave of attraction hit so hard that it nearly knocked him off his feet. His fingers tightened on hers for a second, and he wanted…

He let go and took a quick step back. No. No way. He couldn't let that happen.

For a moment, Annabel thought the buzzing was part of that crazy spark that had leaped between her and Travis. Then she realized it was her cell phone.

Murmuring an excuse, she turned away from Travis, yanking the cell phone from her pocket, and answered, trying not to let her feelings of relief show in her voice.

"Pastor Tim, hello." Pastor Tim Gunnel probably wanted to know if she had all the animals lined up for the Nativity. She sent an annoyed glance toward Toby, who seemed to glare back. "If this is about the animals for the pageant—"

"I'm sure you have that well in hand." Pastor Tim sounded more confident than she felt. "Actually, I have a favor to ask."

"Anything." Her minister had been a rock when the Christmas wedding she'd planned so meticulously didn't happen. If he needed a favor, he had it.

"I'd like you to put Kyle Morrison in your kids' program. You know who I mean?"

"The Morrison family from church?" Kyle. She scoured her memory, coming up with an image of a fourth grader with a stubborn set to his chin and a quick temper. "I don't know him very well, but if you think he'd benefit…"

She left the statement open. Pastor Tim wouldn't break confidentiality, but if she was to help the child, she'd need to know something about the situation.

"I hope so." He blew out his breath in a sigh. "I've had the parents in here regularly, and I've tried to talk with Kyle, but I haven't gotten anywhere." She could hear the worry in his voice. "He's been getting into fights at school, his grades are falling and he's run away twice at least. The parents are at the end of their rope."

"Are they getting professional help?" She leaned against a stall.

"They're reluctant to do that. Afraid of making matters worse. You know how parents can be in this situation."

She did. Afraid of some imaginary stigma attached to having a child who needed help. Maybe afraid of what might come out in a clinical setting.

"I know it's not much to go on," Pastor Tim admitted, "but you've had such success in getting kids to open up once they're working around the animals. Will you try?"

"You know I will. Do you want me to make the arrangements with the parents?"

"I'll do that. Thanks, Annabel. I knew I could count on you."

After she ended the call, she stood for a moment, staring down at the cell phone. Pastor Tim had sent troubled children to her program before, and she had a lot of respect for his judgment. If he thought she could help, she'd do her best.

Guide me, Father. She breathed a silent prayer. *Help me to see how I can help this child. And open his heart to You.*

She slid the phone back into her pocket, feeling comforted, and turned to Travis.

He had gone back to the donkey, talking to him in a low, calming voice. He wasn't paying any attention to her, and she watched for a moment, not moving. Liking the easy way he had with the animal, his big hands moving gently as he spread the ointment on, his deep voice quiet and reassuring.

Maybe this wasn't going to be so difficult, having Travis around. He had a gift with animals—that much was sure. And, from a slightly selfish point of view, it might be that occupying herself with show-ing him a good Christmas would help to keep her painful memories at bay.

Travis unclipped the lead lines, holding on to the donkey's halter, and glanced toward her. "Where do you want him?"

Had he caught her staring at him? She could feel the warmth rush to her cheeks and tried to ignore it.

"Let's put him in the small paddock by himself for now. I like to keep newcomers isolated at first."

Travis fell into step with her, leading the donkey. Outside the barn, she opened the gate leading into the paddock. Travis shooed the donkey in and closed the gate. For a moment they stood side by side, leaning on the gate rail, watching as Toby, after a wary look around, dropped his head and began cropping grass.

"Thanks for finishing up. I didn't want to put off that call. The minister from our church has a boy he wants me to work with, and I thought…" She let that trail off, realizing that Travis was looking at her in confusion.

"Sorry," she said. "Let me start again. I'm getting as bad as my mamma is, babbling away as if you know all about what I do here."

"I know you work with abused and abandoned animals." He jerked a nod toward the pasture. "What else?"

"Peaceable Farm runs a program for kids who are at risk. Actually, that's how I first became acquainted with Sam. He was in one of my early groups."

Travis's dark brows had drawn together. "What kind of risk?"

She'd expected him to ask about the program, but instead he'd zeroed in on the children.

"Some of them come from homes where there's addiction or abuse. Some are acting out in different ways—withdrawn, behavioral problems, getting into trouble at school, running away. Some are learning disabled or physically disabled."

She was flooded with the enthusiasm she always felt when she explained her lifework to someone new, someone interested.

"You see, we've found that involving these children with animals, especially hurting or abandoned animals, can really help them. They start accepting responsibility for a helpless creature, and that helps them to heal."

She had the sudden feeling that Travis had withdrawn. He hadn't moved an inch physically, his hand still inches from hers on the weathered gate. But the icy look in his eyes set her at a distance.

"What's the matter?" The question came out involuntarily.

"You can't help what's wrong with an abused kid by letting him play with animals." The words came out harshly, like a blow in the face.

Her chin went up. "That's not it at all. We have a board of qualified professionals who help us decide on a suitable approach for each child. This isn't just random playtime. Abused children—"

"Abused children need to be taken away from their abusers." He flung the words at her from across what seemed a wide chasm. "They need to see those people punished."

"That's not—"

The crunch of gravel interrupted her, and she caught her breath, trying to regain her composure.

"The children are here for the after-school program. Maybe we'd better have this conversation later. Excuse me." She spun, not looking at him, and marched off toward the van.

She ought to be used to people not understanding the value of her program. She had a calm, reasoned approach to dealing with them. She'd been anything but calm with Travis.

She didn't want to think about why. She smiled and waved as kids came tumbling out of the van. Their arrival had interrupted the quarrel. But it hadn't ended it.

Chapter Three

It was Sunday morning, and Travis was still haunted by his reaction to that encounter with Annabel's kids' program on Thursday. He should have forgotten about it by now, but he couldn't.

If he'd known about it ahead of time—well, no point going back. He just had to find a way to escape any further involvement. With those kids. Maybe with Annabel, too.

He fell into step with Hugh and Miz Callie as they walked toward the church. The elderly woman looked up at him, smiling, her blue eyes bright.

"You haven't forgotten you're coming out to the beach house for Sunday dinner, now, have you?"

"No, ma'am. I'm looking forward to it."

"Good. Looks as if we're going to have a nice day for it." She squinted at the sunlight reflecting from the white steeple that topped the church. "Annabel can take you for a walk on the beach."

She seemed to assume that Annabel was the one designated to entertain him. Given the mix of feelings he had every time he looked at Annabel, that wasn't the best of ideas, but he could hardly argue with an elderly lady.

"I guess this is the church where the Living Nativity is going to be?" he asked, slipping away from the subject of walks on the beach with Annabel.

"Sure is." She gestured toward a stack of lumber on the lawn that spread between the white-columned church and a red-brick building that must be some sort of annex, judging by the children who were streaming into it.

"Looks as if they have a little building to do," Hugh commented.

"Careful." Annabel, walking ahead of them with her mother, tossed the word over her shoulder. "I hear Pastor Tim is looking for volunteers."

The teasing that erupted between her and Hugh gave Travis an excuse to study Annabel. Dressed for church in crisp gray slacks and a coral sweater set, she looked just as pretty as she had in jeans and that favorite flannel shirt of hers.

Was he imagining it, or was there a bit more coolness in her manner toward him since he'd said what he thought about her program? Probably. She hadn't spoken of it since then, and neither had he. He wouldn't have said as much as he did if he hadn't been caught by surprise.

Or if it hadn't been Annabel. He might as well admit that she had a gift for getting to him.

They walked through the double doors to the sanctuary, and he found himself filing into the pew next to Annabel. She sat down, turning to him with a little more warmth in her expression.

"It's beautiful, isn't it?" she said softly. "I never feel as if Christmas is coming until I see the church decorated."

He nodded, taking in the interior of the sanctuary. He'd been surprised by how plain and simple it was, with its white columns marching down the rows of white wooden pews. Garlands wound around the columns, and the windowsills blossomed with greens and candles. The fresh scent of pine filled the air.

"I guess you've gone to church here a long time."

"Since birth," she agreed. "We were all baptized right up there." She nodded toward the front of the sanctuary.

Hugh leaned across her. "I still say the pastor mixed up the two of you. You were really baptized Amanda."

"Stop that." She elbowed him in the ribs. "You were only four at the time. What do you know about it?"

Mrs. Bodine sent a frown down the pew at her offspring. "You children behave in church, y'heah?"

Annabel leaned back, her sleeve brushing his.

"Mamma's been saying that ever since I can remember," she murmured. "If we didn't give her a reason to do it once in a while, she'd be disappointed."

"You're lucky." The words were out before he reflected that once again he'd said more to Annabel than he intended.

She fixed that wide blue gaze on him. "Didn't you have siblings?"

That wasn't what he'd meant, but he seized on it. "I was an only child." Good thing, as it turned out. If he'd had a kid brother or sister to try to protect...

The minister took his place behind the pulpit, saving Travis from the danger of having Annabel question him about his family.

He got through the service by watching Annabel, standing when she did, sitting when she did. Not that a worship service was totally unfamiliar. The second foster family he'd been with had been great churchgoers.

He'd been surprised at the time to find comfort in that. He'd dared to think there might be a Heavenly Father who cared for him, since his own so obviously didn't.

It hadn't lasted, of course. He'd been moved again. The Robinsons could have fought to keep him, but they hadn't. One place followed another, and whatever faith he'd tried to cling to had been lost in the shuffle.

He'd gotten along fine without it. The coast guard was all he needed.

Still, he couldn't deny that he was touched by the service. The music, the prayers, the pastor's resonant voice when he talked about the peace of Christmas… that would touch anyone short of Scrooge.

And when he saw the sheen of tears in Annabel's eyes as they stood to sing the final carol, a wave of tenderness swept over him that scared him.

The last prayer was spoken, the service ended and the family moved from the pew and started toward the doors. He stood back, letting Hugh go between him and Annabel. That was safer.

But she paused, obviously looking for him, when she reached the spot where the minister stood greeting people as they left the service. She caught his sleeve and pulled him toward her.

"Pastor Tim, I'd like to introduce Lieutenant Travis McCall. He's a friend of Luke's, just transferred here from Alaska. Travis, Pastor Tim Gunnel."

Travis found his hand clasped in a solid grip as the lean, graying, middle-aged man surveyed him. "You're welcome here, Travis. I hope we'll be seeing a lot of you. I understand you're giving Annabel a hand out at the farm."

"Yes, sir." News certainly did travel fast. "Thank you."

Should he say something nice about the service?

He wasn't sure of the etiquette, so it was probably better to say too little than too much.

"Good service, Pastor Tim." Hugh reached over to grasp the man's hand, and Travis was glad to have that probing gaze turned on someone else.

"Hugh, you're just the man I wanted to see." Pastor Tim clasped him firmly by the arm, as if Hugh might make a break for it. "I was hoping I could convince you to take over building the stable for the Nativity. You will, won't you?"

Even Hugh's composure faltered a little at the pastor's confidence. "Well, I'm not sure I..."

"He'd be happy to." Hugh's father, looming behind him, answered for him. "We'll all give him a hand. It's a pleasure."

"Right," Hugh echoed, and Travis wasn't sure how he felt about it. "We'll handle it."

Once they were out on the sidewalk, Annabel grinned at her brother. "Told you so," she said.

"Oh, well, it's not too much work, I guess. If my baby sister can provide the animals and Amanda can direct the thing, I guess I can put in some labor." Hugh glanced at him, eyebrows lifting. "What do you say, Travis? You want to give us a hand?"

"I'm game." No one could blame him for spending less time in Annabel's company if he was helping Hugh with the stable, could they?

"Good man." Hugh clapped his shoulder. "How about Tuesday afternoon? I'm free then."

"Fine by me." What could be better? That would get him safely away from the farm when the kids were there.

"Not Tuesday, Hugh." Annabel broke in. "Can't you do it some other time? I was counting on Travis's help with the kids. Sam has his GED prep course then, so he won't be around." She turned to Travis, putting her hand on his arm. "You don't mind, do you?"

"Well, I…" It was awfully hard to say no with those blue eyes looking at him so pleadingly. "I guess I can—"

"Might have known," Hugh said with mock bitterness. "Don't let the twins fool you with that helpless little female act. They've been getting what they want that way since they were two."

"I do not play the helpless female," Annabel retorted. "And if you don't watch it I'll sic Amanda on you. See how brave you are against the two of us."

Hugh held up his hands in surrender. "I give. You can have him on Tuesday. Maybe he can give me a hand on Wednesday afternoon, if that suits you."

Travis nodded. Annabel and her siblings obviously enjoyed their mock battles, and after just a few days around the Bodine clan, he was beginning to understand what had given Luke the easy confidence that marked everything he did.

But the bottom line was that Travis would be helping Annabel with those kids, and he wasn't at all sure he could keep from speaking his mind about it.

"You really didn't need to help with the cleanup after dinner. You're a guest, after all, although we've been putting you to work like one of the family."

The afternoon sun slanted across the deck at the beach house, sparkling on the waves. Annabel stood next to Travis, wondering if she had the nerve to say the thing that lay at the back of her mind.

"It was my pleasure." Travis leaned his elbows on the railing, looking down at the group playing softball on the beach. "Tell me again who everyone is so I don't call anybody by the wrong name."

"They wouldn't mind if you did," she assured him.

Travis was an odd mixture of professional confidence and a sort of shy diffidence where her family was concerned. She sometimes caught him watching them as if he studied creatures from another planet.

"You know my brother Hugh. And that's Adam, my cousin." She pointed to her tall cousin, who was bent over the small boy who would soon be his stepson, helping him hit the ball with a fat plastic bat. "Cathy, his fiancée, and her little boy, Jamie. And you've met my cousin Georgia, her husband, Matt, and their little girl, Lindsay." She grinned. "Miz Callie took pity on you and didn't invite the whole crew today. She said if we didn't introduce you gradually to the Bodines, you'd probably run right back to Alaska."

He looked down at her, a smile crinkling the corners of his eyes. "I'm not that easily scared."

Except by the troubled children in her after-school program, it seemed to her. She'd been thinking it for the past several days, but she hadn't been able to make up her mind to say anything. It wasn't any of her business why he'd reacted so strongly, was it? Still…

"You know, there's somethin' else you don't need to do, besides cleaning up dishes." She took the plunge without giving herself time to second-guess. "I know I put you on the spot, but you don't need to help me with the after-school kids. I can round up someone else to lend a hand if you…"

She let that sentence die, because Travis was shaking his head.

"Don't. I'll do it." He paused. His gaze was fixed on the ballplayers, but she didn't think he saw them. "I just wasn't prepared, that's all. It'll be fine."

There was a trace of something…doubt, maybe… under the words, and that troubled her. She put her hand on his arm, and it was so warm and strong that she wanted to snatch her hand away. But she didn't.

"Are you sure?" She looked into his face, trying to see what was in his heart.

He put his hand over hers, clasping it so firmly that her breath caught. "I'm sure." His deep voice had roughened.

For a moment, she thought he was going to say something else, maybe even to tell her what lay behind his attitude. But Hugh hailed them from the beach.

"Hey, Annabel. Travis. Come on down. We need some help beating the small fry."

Travis drew his hand away from hers and returned Hugh's wave. "Ready to go down?"

"You go ahead." It took an effort to keep her voice even. "I'll get Miz Callie."

But he'd barely disappeared down the stairs of the deck when Miz Callie stepped through the sliding door. Annabel gave her grandmother a stern look.

"Miz Callie, you weren't eavesdropping, now, were you?"

"'Course not, child." Miz Callie joined her at the rail, putting her arm around Annabel's waist. "I just didn't want to interrupt when y'all were getting so close, that's all."

Annabel could feel the heat in her cheeks. "We weren't…I mean, we were just talking about the kids' program, that's all. He seemed a little bothered by it, and I wanted him to feel free to back off."

"He didn't, did he?" Miz Callie smiled when Annabel shook her head. "I didn't think so. That boy has got a strong sense of duty. And a good heart to go with it, if I'm any judge."

Annabel gave her a squeeze. "You're the best judge of people I've ever met, Miz Callie. I'll take your word for it."

"Seems to me you were well on your way to finding out for yourself what makes Travis McCall tick." Miz Callie's eyes twinkled.

"I...I'm just trying to make him feel welcome. There's nothing more to it."

Miz Callie cocked her head. "Why not?"

"What?" She blinked, staring at her grandmother.

"You heard me, child. Seems like the two of you might really hit it off, if you didn't back away every time a man gets close."

She was used to the frontal attack from her sister, but she hadn't expected it from her grandmother. She stared down at her hand, which was clenched on the railing. "Truth is, I'm scared of getting too close."

"Annabel, sugar, it's been two years. Don't you think it's time to let your former fiancé go? Foster showed he wasn't worthy of you when he walked away."

"I have let him go." It was true. She barely thought of Foster anymore. "But it seems like I just don't have the courage to take that risk of loving someone again."

There was a little silence once she'd said the

words. Then Miz Callie patted her hand. "I know, child. I know your confidence took a pretty hard knock. But you have to start trusting your judgment again sometime. Seems like now might be a good time."

She shook her head, her throat tight. "I wish I could."

"There, now, it's all right." Miz Callie patted her again. "I just don't want you to give up."

"I'll try."

Miz Callie put her small, still-strong hand against Annabel's cheek, as she had when Annabel was a small child. "You do that. And I reckon you're going to find that when you need the courage enough, God is going to give it to you."

"Are you ready?" Travis asked the question, but he had a feeling that he was the one who wasn't ready for this.

The little girl in the wheelchair smiled, nodding. The red helmet she wore bobbled with the nod, and she raised her arms to him.

"Mandie loves Dolly." The teenage girl Annabel had assigned to help him held the head of the black-and-white pinto pony. "She'll do fine, won't you, sugar?"

The child's mother, holding the handles of the chair, nodded, as well.

His fears allayed a bit, Travis bent, lifting the little

girl in his arms. She was so light that it seemed she could float right up onto the saddle. Travis settled her into place, and she gripped the saddle horn with both hands. Casey, the teenager, fastened the safely harness around the child deftly.

Maybe Annabel had exaggerated a bit when she'd said she needed him today. She had three teenage girls, who were obviously practiced helpers, and several parents had come with their children. Still, he could understand that she might want to have another adult around who understood the animals.

He grasped Mandie the way Annabel had shown him, countering the child's tendency to slip to one side. Casey went to Dolly's head, sending him an inquiring glance.

"Okay?"

He nodded. Dolly moved off at a slow walk, and he kept pace with her. Mandie, clutching the saddle tightly, seemed to concentrate on the pony's head, bobbing in front of her—trying to keep her balance, he realized. Exerting as much effort and concentration on that simple act as he might landing a helicopter on a ship's deck at night. The thought wrenched at his heart

He smiled at her. "Doing great, Mandie. Just great. Let yourself feel Dolly's movements under you."

"I won't fall," she said, maybe to reassure herself.

"No, you won't. Dolly's been doing this for years,

I bet, and she knows exactly what she's doing. Right, Casey?"

"Right." Casey tossed a smile back over her shoulder at the child. With her silky red hair cut in the latest style and her pert, pretty face, she looked as if she ought to be at cheerleading practice instead of tramping around a soggy field, but here she was.

They made a slow circuit of the paddock and then another one. He could feel Mandie relaxing, although she had to have been getting tired, judging by her grip on the saddle.

Now what? Annabel hadn't told him how long the child could or should do this.

"What do you think, Mandie? Are you up for one more time around today?" Casey came to his rescue.

Mandie's thin hands tightened, and she jerked a nod. They set off on a third circuit. He could feel the child's exhaustion now as she leaned against his arm, and he gripped her more firmly.

"Doing great, Mandie. We're almost there. You can do it." He leaned closer to the pony, trying to give the child as much security as possible. A flash of concern went through him. If this was too much for her…

But she hung on, and when they reached the starting point she gave him a broad grin. Casey and her mother broke into applause as Travis lifted her back into the chair.

"See that? You did it. Dolly would clap if she could. Give me five." He held his palm close to her hand.

The tap of her hand nearly missed, but her grin more than made up for it, and the lump in his throat was so huge that he couldn't have said another thing.

"Great job, Mandie."

He hadn't heard Annabel approach; he'd been so focused on the child, but there she was. "One of the barn cats just brought her new kittens out. Would you like to see them?"

Mandie nodded, her small face beaming, and her mother turned the chair.

"Bless you," the mother said softly, glancing at him as she wheeled the chair away.

He glanced at Annabel. "I take back any doubts I had. That's definitely worth it."

Annabel's blue eyes were bright with tears despite her smile. "It is. She's a brave little kid." She shook her head slightly. "Well, don't get too soft, because next comes a test of your patience."

"Not the terrible twosome," Casey said.

"Not only that but we've got a third today." Annabel nodded toward three boys who were being shepherded toward them by another of the helpers. "Todd, Charlie and the new one is Kyle. Behavioral problems. They need firm control, or they'll create havoc." She gave Travis an assessing look. "You ought to be good at that. Use your officer voice."

"I'll try." What kind of behavior problems, he wanted to ask, but Annabel was already striding off, her long braid swinging. He sent a glance at Casey, and she shrugged.

"They're not mean," she said. "Just…active. Very, very active."

He soon saw what she meant. With Kyle on the pony, now on a long lead line walking a circle around Casey, Todd and Charlie apparently were intent on seeing who could annoy him the most. He snatched Charlie from balancing on the top rail of the paddock fence, only to discover that Todd was entangled in brambles and wailing that his mother would kill him if he tore his new shirt. Releasing the boy at the cost of a few scratches to his own hands, Travis turned to discover that Charlie emptied his backpack in search of something, allowing paper to flutter across the grass.

Travis, gritting his teeth, grabbed both of them and marched them to the fence. Annabel had been right—this did require a firm hand.

"Anyone who is not on the pony will police the area. You and you—" he pointed to them "—pick up every scrap of paper between the paddock and the lane or no riding. That's an order."

Apparently intimidated by his tone, they nodded and bent to the task.

Had he been too sharp? Maybe not, judging by their expressions when they came back to him.

"All done, sir." Charlie stood up very straight, as if standing for inspection.

He took his time, looking over what they'd done and then gave them an approving nod. "Good work, men. Now it's Charlie's turn on the pony."

They took turns riding. Kyle, who was apparently the new kid, seemed to fit in all right. He even lost his sullen expression a time or two while he was riding.

The session was finally over, and the three boys headed toward the barn without arguing.

"Good job," Casey said to him. "They have to groom the pony now. I can get them started on that if you need a break."

Maybe she'd noticed the fact that his eyes had been drawn to the nearest pasture, where Annabel was introducing several children to the smallest of the goats. He stood watching for a moment. Gentleness seemed to flow through her every movement, expressing itself in her quiet voice and soft smile. If this was really Peaceable Farm, it struck him that the peace started with Annabel.

A shout from the barn jerked his attention away from her. He ran toward the sound, into the barn, taking precious seconds as his eyes adjusted to the dimness after the bright sunlight.

Kyle and Charlie were battling each other, landing

ineffectual punches that probably didn't hurt them much. Still, the ferocity on their faces was alarming. Todd stood back, looking scared, and Casey tried to keep the two boys away from Dolly's hooves.

Travis waded in, grabbing the combatants by the collars and yanking them to their feet.

"What's going on here?" he demanded.

"Kyle wouldn't let me have a turn." Charlie's red face slowly returned to a normal color under Travis's stern gaze. "And then he punched me and knocked me down."

Travis glanced at Casey, who nodded, agreeing with that assessment.

Releasing Charlie, he turned to Kyle. "What do you say, Kyle? That how it went down?"

Kyle's face set in stubborn lines. He jerked away from Travis, his hands doubled into fists. He didn't strike out. He stood, tension in every line of his small body, and for a moment, there was an expression in his eyes that made Travis's stomach twist.

It didn't take much. Just the smallest leap of imagination could put Travis into that kid's body, looking that way. Tense. Ready for what was coming. Knowing it would be a blow.

Chapter Four

"Look, look at the carolers!" Lindsay leaned forward as far as her seat belt would allow in the backseat of Annabel's car. "Look, cousin Annabel!"

"I see them." Annabel slowed the car still more and exchanged a smile with Travis.

The carolers, like all the displays at the James Island Christmas Festival, had been created from colored lights—thousands of lights, turning the park into a magical celebration of Christmas in the early evening dark.

"I can't see, cousin Annabel. I'm on the wrong side." Jamie's complaint was an echo of things she'd said herself as a child, packed into the car with her three siblings.

"The next one's on your side," Travis pointed out. "Look. What is it?"

Diverted, both children craned toward the windows, exchanging guesses as the next display came into view.

"Good job averting a battle," she murmured to Travis. "You're not bad with kids."

He shook his head. "I have to say, this display is awesome. They do this every year?"

"Every year since I can remember. It's a holiday tradition."

And it was one she hadn't shared with Foster. Her former fiancé had enjoyed the holiday social whirl, but for him, that hadn't included something as simple as a drive through the park to admire the lights. Doing it now seemed to take some of the sting of memories away. Her plan to keep herself busy with Travis's entertainment was working.

She glanced at Travis. He'd swung around to look toward the kids in the backseat, putting his hand on the back of her seat and bringing his face closer to hers. He was explaining how one of the lighting effects had been achieved, answering Jamie's questions with the same patience he'd shown when he took Mandie on the pony.

He was one of the good guys. Her heart twisted a little. Maybe she wasn't being entirely fair, using him to help her get through the holiday season.

Still, Travis didn't know that her motives for doing this were mixed. And Luke *had* asked her to entertain him. So what harm did it do?

She glanced at her watch as she pulled into the parking lot. "Okay, kids, it's almost time for the bonfire and stories. Then we'll see the rest of the lights."

"Will there be hot chocolate?" Lindsay asked. "My mamma said there would."

"I'm sure there will be." She unlatched her seat belt. "Let's see if we can find it."

They ushered the kids quickly from the parking lot and started down the path that led to the bonfire area. Lindsay and Jamie hurried ahead, holding hands, and Travis walked with her, his eyes on the kids.

"Looks like Jamie's limping a little." His voice expressed concern. "He didn't get hurt getting out of the car, did he?"

"Jamie had some congenital birth defects. He's had a rough time of it, poor little guy. But he had his last surgery a few months ago, and they say he's going to be absolutely fine." Her heart clenched at the memory of how they'd all prayed their way through that operation. "It's going to be a happy Christmas for them—maybe the best in a long time."

"Sounds like he's had a rough time of it." Travis frowned slightly. "I'm surprised their folks were willing to let us bring them tonight. I'd think they would want to do it themselves."

"Oh, they will. No one is content to see the lights just once." Travis didn't need to know that she'd used him as an excuse to borrow the children for the evening.

They'd reached the bonfire circle, and for a few moments, she was totally occupied in getting the kids their cookies and hot chocolate and finding seats where a costumed storyteller waited to entertain them.

When she rejoined Travis, who stood waiting at the edge of the circle of light cast by the bonfire, he handed her a cup of hot chocolate. "I figured you weren't too old to enjoy this, too."

She wrapped her hands around the cup and inhaled the sweet aroma. "No way. I'm never going to outgrow some things, and hot chocolate with marshmallows on a chilly night is one of them."

"Chilly," he repeated, a laugh in his voice. "This is downright balmy, if you ask me."

"Only if you just arrived from Alaska," she retorted. "Down here if it drops below sixty we haul out the heavy jackets."

He nodded, smiling, but she had a sense that his mind was on something other than the light teasing. "I guess you can work with the kids all winter, then."

"Pretty much. Last year I had to cancel a few sessions when it was cold and wet, but for the most part, we go ahead with it."

He was silent for a moment. What was he thinking that carved those deep lines in his forehead? She'd been congratulating herself that he'd gotten over his qualms about her program, but maybe he hadn't.

"Is something wrong?" She asked the question, not sure she wanted an answer.

His strong jaw seemed to harden. "That kid, Kyle. What's his story?"

"Kyle Morrison? I don't know much yet. That was his first session with us. Pastor Tim referred him."

"You must know something." His gaze probed her face, as if he looked for answers.

She wouldn't share anything confidential with Travis, of course, but if he were to help with the kids, he had to be told something. And the truth of it was that she didn't know much to tell—not yet.

"Pastor Tim asked me to take him. They're members of our church, and Pastor Tim is counseling them. Kyle has been having problems at school, and he's run away twice. I don't think it's anything too serious. His dad travels a lot on business, and I wondered if Kyle might be trying to get his attention."

Travis crumpled his cup and tossed it into the nearest trash can. He turned to her, his expression uncompromising. "I think the kid is being abused."

For a moment, she could only gape at him. "Abused? But…there's never been any suggestion of that. Pastor Tim would have the authorities involved in a split second if he had any reason to suspect it. Really, Travis, I can't believe that."

"Can't?" He spit out the word. "Or won't? Are you sure you're not affected by the fact that they're members of your church?"

"I'm not that naive." She glared back at him, careful to keep her voice low. "I'm the one who has been working with these kids, remember? Do you think I don't know that abuse spans every segment of society? Of course it's possible, but there hasn't been any hint of that."

"I hope you're right." But his tone sounded as if he thought she was wrong. "I'd just like to know if Kyle's bad times happen to coincide with when his father comes back from his trips."

Travis really ought to stay away from Annabel Bodine, given the fact that every time he was near her, he said more than he should. But here he was, helping her to decorate her parents' boat for something called a Christmas Boat Parade.

From his perch in the prow of the cabin cruiser, where he was fastening a string of lights, he had a good view of Annabel. She sat on the deck, engaged in untangling a bird's nest of lights. Seeming to feel his gaze on her, she looked up and smiled.

That smile was enough to set off warning bells in his heart. He couldn't even kid himself that he was hanging out with Annabel because of his promise to his buddy. Something about her drew him, as if that warmth of hers reached out and latched on to his heart.

Giving in to the feeling would be a mistake. He

knew that, didn't he? He drove a staple into place with a little-more-than-necessary energy.

"I declare, if I knew who put these lights away in such a mess, I'd give them a piece of my mind." Annabel began coiling the string she'd been working on. "Hugh Bodine, are you responsible for this?" She had to raise her voice to be heard over the Christmas carols Hugh had been playing.

"What?" Hugh popped his head up from where he lay, trying to hook up some speakers. "Whatever it is, I didn't do it."

Travis couldn't help but smile. "That was the right answer, even if he didn't hear the question."

"As if he'd admit it," she said. "He and Luke always blamed each other for anything that went wrong."

"So tell me about this boat parade," he said, more to head off another spat between the siblings than because he cared. "What's it all about?"

"You've never seen a boat parade?" She sat back on her heels. With her forest-green windbreaker over a red turtleneck, she looked like a Christmas ornament herself, especially with her cheeks rosy from the breeze off the water.

He shook his head. "I grew up inland."

"Well, I suppose it's like any Christmas parade, except it's on the water. Anybody who wants to can decorate their boats with lights, and we sail down the Cooper River, all the way past the Battery. You should see the people who line up to watch. When I was a kid, I couldn't wait until I was old enough to help. Seeing the lighted boats going downriver in the evening, Christmas carols playing…"

"If I can't get these speakers fixed, there might not be any carols," Hugh interrupted. "Daddy should be here. He can fix anything electrical."

"If he doesn't shock himself first," Annabel said. "Anyway, it doesn't matter. If everybody has music playing, I have to admit it clashes a bit."

"Remember the year Luke rigged our speakers to play that rock 'n' roll Christmas song Daddy hated?" Hugh grinned. "Now Daddy checks every last thing before he lets us take the boat out."

Hugh's cell phone rang just then, and he turned away to answer.

Annabel brought a string of lights to Travis.

"Here. I'll hold while you staple." Judging by the reminiscent smile that curved her lips, she was still thinking of Christmases past.

And the more he was around her, the harder he found it to hold back memories of his own painful Christmases.

Hugh slid his cell phone into his pocket. "Hey, Bel, I've got to go. D'you two mind finishin' up?"

"I guess not. If we don't get it all done, we'll put stuff away, at least." She glanced up at Travis's face. "Is that okay with you?"

"Fine." He hoped that sounded enthusiastic enough.

He was their guest. He had to fall in with what they wanted to do, didn't he?

They worked a while longer in silence except for the music. Annabel hummed along softly.

"You people do like celebrating Christmas, don't you?"

She tilted her head, looking at him a little quizzically. "I guess so. Doesn't everyone?"

He shrugged, not quite willing to answer that.

Annabel stretched out a strand of wire, frowning at it. "I guess we kind of railroaded you into helping. If you're tired of this—"

"No, of course not." He didn't want to offend anybody. Or did Annabel mean that she wanted to leave?

But she just nodded and went on with the work. "I guess we do all get a little sappy about the family celebration—you know, all the silly little traditions families build up around the holidays."

No, he didn't know, but he wasn't going to admit that to her. "I guess you have plenty of perfect Christmas memories."

She seemed to consider that. "I don't know that they were always that perfect, although Mamma surely did try to make them that way. I mean, there were the years when Daddy was stationed someplace far away and couldn't get home for Christmas. Everybody tried to put a good face on it, but it wasn't easy."

Military families had to put up with that, but it must be hard. "I'm sorry. I didn't mean to bring up a sad memory."

"It's all right. I just didn't want you to think we claimed to be perfect. After what happened—" She stopped, quite suddenly, as if whatever she was going to say was too difficult. "Anyway, it'll be a little bittersweet this year, with Luke not home."

He nodded. What had she been about to say before changing her mind? He'd probably never know.

"Sorry. I guess I'm a pretty poor substitute."

"Don't say that." The words burst out of her as she looked up, putting her hand on his. "Please don't think that. We love having you here. It's not—"

He touched her lips with his fingers, hushing her, indescribably moved by the caring in her face. "Don't." The word came out in a murmur. "I wasn't…"

He didn't mean to do it—didn't even think about it. But her lips were warm against his fingertips, and there was so much caring in her eyes that rational thought slid away. And then he was kissing her, his arms going around her, and it seemed the most natural thing in the world.

Her thoughts tumbling crazily, Annabel responded to the kiss, her hands grasping Travis's arms, feeling his strength and caring.

He drew back after an endless moment, and the cool breeze off the water touched her lips. And in that instant, all the doubts rushed in. She couldn't do this—couldn't get involved with anyone, couldn't trust her own emotions, not now, not when...

"I'm sorry." He let her go carefully, seeming to withdraw. "I shouldn't have done that. I didn't mean to upset you."

"You didn't." She blinked, realizing that tears were spilling over onto her cheeks. She wiped them away with her fingers.

Poor Travis. He probably thought she was crazy, bursting into tears because he'd kissed her.

"I'm sorry. I'm acting like an idiot." She managed a watery smile.

"No problem." His tone was casual, but she heard the hurt and embarrassment beneath it.

"Look, I...we can't leave it like that." She caught his hand, drew him down next to her on the bench seat. The marina was empty. Darkness drew in quickly on a December evening on the water. No one could see or hear.

Travis sat, but he looked as if he were ready to spring up and stride away. "You don't have to explain anything to me."

"Yes, I do." She took a breath. "It's not you. I wasn't upset or annoyed or...or anything."

She'd enjoyed the kiss, but maybe it was better if she didn't say that. She took another breath, trying to steady herself.

"Two years ago I was engaged to be married. On

Christmas Eve. He…broke it off right before the wedding. Didn't quite leave me waiting at the altar, but it was close enough." She had to get this out quickly or she wouldn't manage it.

"He must have been crazy."

She blinked, meeting his gaze. "I don't think he saw it that way." She tried not to picture Foster's face when he told her he couldn't go through with it. "It was the right thing to do. I know that now. We couldn't get married if one of us wasn't sure. His decision was just so hard to accept."

It had flattened her, and that was the truth of the matter. She couldn't understand why she hadn't seen it coming. Or maybe she'd been too busy with all the details of the wedding to pay enough attention to the groom. That wasn't a very pleasant thought.

"Anyway, I guess my emotions still run pretty high at this time of the year. The silliest things remind me. I don't want to…to…"

She lost her forward momentum then, and she couldn't manage to say anything else.

She didn't want to risk getting involved with anyone else. She stared down at her linked fingers, twisting together. Now she'd made Travis uncomfortable, blurting all that out. She'd made a mess of this for sure.

Travis's hand closed over hers, gripping them in a firm squeeze. "It's okay. I understand. It's just… bad timing." His chocolate-brown eyes seemed to darken. "Christmas can be an emotional time for people—especially when our lives change."

She knew without asking what he was thinking. Luke had told her about the woman Travis had been in love with—about how her love hadn't been strong enough to survive his accident.

She couldn't say anything about that. Or could she?

She took a deep breath, murmuring a silent prayer. "I know that coming here is a big change in your life. You're probably missing all the friends you left behind in Alaska. If you were there, you'd be celebrating Christmas with them."

He was silent for a long moment. He still held her hands clasped in his. Maybe he'd forgotten that he was holding them.

"I'd been looking forward to Christmas up there." He said the words carefully, as if they might break. "Maybe the first time I was really excited about it. But after the accident…" He stopped. "Luke told you about that, didn't he?"

"Yes. He said you put yourself at risk to take care of your crew."

His cheeks reddened a little under his tan, just visible in the reflection of the Christmas lights. "He would have done the same. So would Adam, Hugh or your father, for that matter. That's what we do."

"I know." Her throat was tight. "I've been around

the coast guard all my life. But I still admire you for it."

He shook his head. "The thing was that after I got well enough to return to duty…" He stopped, as if not sure he wanted to go on.

"You requested a transfer." She finished the thought for him, wanting to help. Wanting him to keep on talking but afraid to mention the woman unless he did.

He took a deep breath. "Luke told you about Linda, didn't he?"

"I'm sorry. He wasn't gossiping, honestly. He thought…" She stopped, not sure what had been behind Luke's telling her. "Maybe he thought I'd understand, because I'd been through it."

A muscle twitched at the corner of his firm lips. If she'd made him angry at Luke, she'd done more harm than good.

"He might have been right about that." Travis stared down at their clasped hands, but she wasn't sure he saw them. "I thought what I had with Linda was the real thing. That this Christmas I'd be with someone I loved, and—"

He stopped, so abruptly that she knew there were things he didn't want to tell her.

"Well, anyway, looks like we're in the same boat." He gave an unconvincing smile and reached over the railing to pat the hull. "In more ways than one."

If he wanted to make light of it, all she could do

was go along with him, even though it made her heart ache for his pain.

"That's us, all right," she said lightly. "A pair of losers in the game of love."

"So, what happened between us…we'll forget about it. We'll go back to being friends. Okay?"

She forced herself to meet his gaze and found nothing but friendship there. She let out a sigh of relief. "Okay. I'd hate to think I'd lost that."

She tried to smile. She tried not to think that she might want more from Travis than he was willing to give.

Chapter Five

Annabel did her best to focus on introducing the youngest children to the new kittens, teaching them to treat the tiny creatures with gentleness. For children whose own lives hadn't been marked by much of that, it could be harder than it sounded.

"Easy," she cautioned. "Patches will let you touch her kittens, but you mustn't be rough with them. She won't let you do that." Patches had allowed her now-lively kittens to be brought out into a patch of sunlight outside the barn, but she circled them, alert for trouble.

"Why not?" Joshua, one of the six-year-olds, always had to know why.

"Because she's their mamma. She takes care of them."

"Like my grammy takes care of me," he said, nodding, apparently satisfied.

"That's right." She knew Joshua's story. His mother

was in a rehab facility, not for the first time, but his grandmother, an iron-willed woman, wouldn't let her grandchildren suffer for that.

She glanced toward the barn. Travis and Sam were showing Kyle and the other two boys how to groom Toby, the donkey. Toby had made great strides recently. Travis, on the other hand…

Not surprisingly, he'd avoided having any conversation with her that dipped below the surface since that night on the boat. She could understand that. She'd felt much the same after telling him about her almost-wedding.

Not that either of them had really said all that much. They were alike in that—private people who didn't show their pain readily.

In contrast with his, her private grief didn't seem to amount to all that much. Her mind winced away from the pain he'd endured. To lie in a hospital bed or struggle in therapy, afraid as he must have been that he'd never fly again…that was bad enough. To have the person he loved walk away at a time like that would have been devastating.

So it was important not to think too much about that kiss. It couldn't have meant anything, and she had to treat it lightly, as Travis was.

"Gently," she cautioned again. She stroked Joshua's dark curly hair, her touch loving. "Like that."

He gave her an engaging grin and petted the small kitten, his grubby hand soft on the fur.

The cat's tail began to twitch, suggesting that she'd had enough.

"Okay, that's it for now." She began scooping kittens back into their basket. Forestalling the inevitable protest, she added quickly, "I'm going to show you how to gather eggs from the chickens. Come along now."

The children at her heels, she walked toward the chicken coop. As she neared the little group around the donkey, she saw that Travis had given Kyle the job of putting ointment on the nearly healed sores.

A tingle of apprehension shivered through her. If Travis's suspicions about Kyle were true, was that really a good idea?

"Sam, would you mind going on an egg hunt with this crew? I'll give Travis a hand with the donkey."

Sam nodded, relinquishing the halter to her. "Come on, guys. But watch the hens. Sometimes they peck." He made a snapping motion with his fingers, making them giggle, and led them off.

Travis didn't seem to pay any attention to her. All of his focus was on Kyle as he guided the boy's hand over the marks.

"Someone hurt him, you see." His voice was gravelly, as if he spoke through a tight throat. "Nobody should do that."

Alarmed, she plunged into the conversation. "Good work, Kyle. Now, I want you boys to scoot along and get Dolly's saddle and bridle. We're going to see how good you are at saddling up."

Predictably, the boys dropped what they were doing and raced for the barn. Travis just looked at her, his dark eyebrows drawing down.

"Afraid of what I might say to him?"

"I hope you have better sense than to bring up your suspicions to Kyle." Her pulse slowly returned to normal. That was exactly what she'd feared.

He turned back to the donkey, taking up the job Kyle had started. "Somebody has to do something."

"I'm not ignoring your judgment about Kyle." She might think he was way off base, but she wouldn't ever ignore anything that had to do with a child's safety and happiness. "I've already talked to Pastor Tim about it."

Travis looked at her then, still frowning. "And what did he say? That it couldn't be true?"

"No, he did not." Anger spurted up, and she tried to get a handle on it. "He took what you said very seriously. But you have to understand that without more to go on, an accusation like that can be disastrous."

"It's disastrous for the child, if it is true."

"I know." Pain shivered through her at the thought, wiping away the anger. "Pastor Tim is consulting with a child psychologist on how best to handle the situation. He can't just blurt out an accusation with no evidence—he'd lose any chance he has of help-ing the family." She reached out to touch Travis's arm, finding it taut with tension. "Pastor Tim will do his part. Our job is to be Kyle's friends—to make this the one place where he might feel comfortable enough and safe enough to tell the truth. You do see that, don't you?"

He was silent for a long moment. Then he swung toward her. "Okay, Annabel. I trust you. We'll do it your way."

His fingers closed over hers. Her heart lurched, as if he'd touched it. She cared about him, she thought, dismayed. She cared about Travis, way too much.

Annabel didn't understand, Travis had decided. How could she? She might know intellectually that people abused their children, but she didn't have the experience to understand why he felt so strongly about Kyle.

He'd pretty much decided that the best thing he could do was stay out of her way, because if he was around her, he wanted to badger her about what Pastor Tim was doing. He wanted to push, to insist, but he'd agreed they'd do it her way.

Staying away from Annabel wasn't working out so well, though. At the moment, on a mild December evening, he stood next to a horse-drawn carriage, waiting to help Annabel give buggy rides as part of the Old Town Mt. Pleasant Christmas Festival.

"Okay, we're all set." Annabel, a bright red stocking cap perched on her head, hurried up to him, waving a handful of brochures. "They're selling the tickets at a central booth, so all we have to do is drive—and talk to the customers, of course."

He gave her a hand up to the high seat. "I'll drive. You talk. You're the one who grew up in Mt. Pleasant. What am I going to tell them about Mt. Pleasant?" Or Christmas, for that matter.

"That sounds fair." Annabel took a deep breath, seeming to settle her nerves. "We're supposed to do a trial run through the streets first, just to be sure we know our routes. Folks will see us and rush to get tickets. That's the idea, anyway."

He glanced at her, wondering if she really was as nervous as she sounded. "What are you worried about? We'll get plenty of business."

The carriage ahead of them moved out, so he released the brake and slapped the lines. The horse, a heavy draft horse named Buddy, moved forward obediently.

"I'm not worried, exactly." Annabel tugged at the red mittens that matched her cap. "Well, maybe I am. I don't think I'm the best person to entertain a bunch of tourists. Or even a buggy load of people I know, come to think of it."

"Why not? You know this area like the back of your hand. You've been telling me about it ever since I arrived, haven't you?"

He slanted an amused glance at her. Annabel was so calm and confident at the farm with the animals or at home with her family. This gave him a different view of her.

"Oh, I know the history, all right. I can tell you that the place on the corner is one of the oldest houses in Mt. Pleasant and that the church in the next block was hit by an errant shell during the battle of Fort Sumter. But that's different than talking to strangers."

"You'll do fine." He took one hand from the lines long enough to pat her arm, touched by this glimpse of insecurity. "Just pretend you're showing me around."

"I'll try." She didn't sound very sure. "But Amanda would do it so much better."

He blinked. "What does Amanda have to do with this? She doesn't know how to drive a horse, does she?"

"Goodness, no." Annabel grinned at the thought. "I meant the talking part. Daddy always says that Amanda never met a stranger. She can walk into a crowd of people she never met, and the next thing you know, someone is telling her his life story."

"That must be a big help to her as a reporter."

They made a right turn onto the next street, and he began to get the route set in his mind. Not difficult at all—the organizers had set it up with all right turns, so they wouldn't be crossing traffic.

"I guess. But she's always been that way, ever since I can remember. Even when we were kids. If we got into trouble, I always counted on Amanda to talk our way out of it. And when Mamma took us out to tea with the older ladies—" a little shiver went through her "—Amanda loved that kind of thing. Getting dressed up and making conversation over tea and cake was her idea of fun. She'd have them eating out of her hand."

"What were you doing while the ladies were eating out of Amanda's hand?"

"Hiding in the corner," she said promptly. "Trying not to be noticed."

A wave of sympathy went through him. He'd always figured Annabel had a perfect childhood. Maybe she had, in comparison to his, but that didn't mean she'd come out unscathed.

"Your mother shouldn't have forced you to go if you hated it that much."

"She thought it would help me get over my shyness." She shrugged. "It was okay, I guess. I always had Amanda, and I could count on her to bear the brunt of it." Her lips twitched. "Amanda never had a shy moment in her life."

He pictured the poised, confident reporter. No, maybe she hadn't. "You liked being a twin?"

"Who wouldn't? Don't get me wrong, I love my brothers. But a sister is special in a way, and having one who's your exact age is wonderful." She gave a little chuckle of laughter. "She'll never admit we're the same age, though. She always has to point out that she's twenty minutes older."

"No downsides to being a twin?" He couldn't imagine what it would be like to have a sibling. He'd always been grateful there hadn't been anyone else to try to protect from Dad's anger. But maybe he'd missed out on something, too.

Annabel seemed to be considering that question. "Well, I suppose it was a little disconcerting to be seen as a unit all the time. Everybody in the family always referred to us as 'the twins' as if we weren't two separate individuals."

"Everyone?" That had to hurt, always being linked to someone else, especially when that someone else was talkative, lively Amanda.

"Not Miz Callie," she said, a trace of surprise in her voice. "I hadn't thought of that until you asked, but Miz Callie always sees each of us as individuals."

"You're lucky in your grandmother." Small wonder they all spoke of Miz Callie with such affection and admiration in their voices.

"I am," Annabel agreed. She tucked her mittened hand into the crook of his arm. "That's enough about me. What about your grandparents? Were you close to them?"

"No." The word came out too sharply. He didn't talk about his family, but he couldn't hurt Annabel's feelings just because it was such a sensitive subject. "I mean, I don't remember them. My mother's parents died when I was small, and my dad's parents…" It took a second before he could go on. "My father fought with everyone, including his family. I don't remember ever meeting them."

He'd never realized how odd that sounded, especially to someone like Annabel, who was surrounded by family. Maybe every kid grew up thinking his life was normal, no matter how odd it was.

If his grandparents had been around, would it have made a difference? Would they have seen what was going on, have intervened to make it better?

He'd never know.

They were nearing the ticket station, and a line of customers already extended down the street. In a moment, this quiet conversation would be over.

He felt the pressure of Annabel's hand on his arm.

"I'm sorry." Her voice filled with warmth and caring—the same warmth and caring that flowed from her to every hurting animal or hurting child. "I didn't realize you had so little family." She squeezed his arm. "You can share ours, you know. They're already crazy about you."

"Thanks." It was just a joke, and he ought to treat it that way. But all Annabel's goodness seemed to be wrapping around his heart, and he couldn't.

He couldn't because he cared about her, and the thought scared him to death.

* * *

"Annabel, are you putting that dough in the pan or playing with it?" Mamma's voice was a little tart, which wasn't unusual late in the evening of the Bodine women's annual Christmas cookie baking.

Mamma had the largest kitchen, so she always offered to host. The room was still crowded, even though they'd overflowed into a table in the family room for icing cookies.

"I'm doing it, Mamma." Annabel focused on rolling the cream cheese dough into tiny balls and pressing them into the miniature muffin pans.

"I'll give you a hand, Bel." Amanda appeared next to her, wiping her hands on a paper towel. "If I have to frost another sugar cookie, I'll scream."

"Just remember how much everybody loves them. Including you." She moved over, giving her twin space to work with her on the pecan tassies.

"I've tasted too much frosting," Amanda admitted. "I went past the sugar rush and straight to exhaustion."

"It's a busy time of year at the paper, isn't it? Why didn't you beg off? Mamma would have understood."

Amanda grinned. "She would not. And anyway, I couldn't stand missing this." She glanced across the kitchen, affection wiping the tired look from her eyes.

"It is a special Christmas tradition." All the aunts,

Mamma, her twin, the female cousins…everybody tied together by bonds of love, blood, family. She couldn't miss it, either. "I'm glad Ross was willing to spare you tonight."

"Ross knows better than to tread on any Bodine family traditions." Worry touched Amanda's face, wrinkling her forehead. "I do wish he and Daddy got along better. I don't know what Daddy's going to say when we set a wedding date."

Despite her hands being sticky, Annabel gave her twin a hug. "He'll be fine. You know that, don't you? Anyway, I think the truth of it is that he and Ross enjoy arguing. I do believe they pick different sides of every issue just for the sake of debating it."

"You might be right at that." Amanda's brow smoothed out. "I hope so, 'cause I have my heart set on a spring wedding, no matter what anybody thinks."

"Oh, Manda." Annabel had to stop and hug her again. "I'm so glad."

"Well, you're my maid of honor, don't forget."

"I won't." She blinked back tears. "We made that promise when we were five, and I'll never forget." They'd attended their first wedding, just barely able to understand what all the fuss was about, but once they'd figured out the roles, they'd agreed.

"Don't say anything, okay? I want to get Daddy in a really good mood before we tell him."

She thought Amanda was worrying unnecessarily, but she nodded her agreement.

"You're okay with this, aren't you? I mean, it doesn't upset you, thinking about my wedding?"

For a moment she actually didn't know what Amanda meant. Then understanding flooded in. "You mean because of Foster? Don't be silly."

"Well, you don't talk about him anymore, but I thought you might still be hurting, especially at this time of year."

"I thought it would bother me," she said the words slowly, trying to understand what had changed. And why. "I mean, I've been over Foster for a while now, but it still hurt." She pressed the last round of dough into the pan. "I guess it was the whole idea that I'd been so wrong about him. I was humiliated, but it was more than that. I thought I couldn't trust my own judgment."

"And now?"

"And now…well, I think I understand myself a little better. Isn't that what Miz Callie always says? That the past is for learning from?"

Amanda nodded. "I guess so. It's just a shame it had to hurt so much."

She thought of Travis, who had surely been hurt more than she had. "Yes. It is."

Amanda picked up the pan that contained the pecan filling and set it where they could both reach it. "Does Travis McCall happen to have anything to do with your recovery, by any chance?"

She wanted to deny it, but her twin would know instantly if she lied. "Maybe," she admitted. "Seeing him pitch in at the farm, fall in with all our crazy family traditions without a whimper…well, I started off entertaining him with the selfish notion of keeping my mind occupied and off Foster, and I ended up comparing Foster to him. And believe me, Foster came in a distant second."

"True, so true." Amanda giggled. "I can't picture Foster getting manure on his shoes or wrestling with a donkey."

"This hasn't been easy for Travis." Now that she'd let herself think about him, she couldn't seem to shut Travis out of her mind. "I mean, coming in to a family like ours, adapting to our traditions, especially when he's facing big changes in his own life…"

"You don't need to convince me." Her twin was looking at her with something speculative in her eyes. "I agree. He's one of the good guys."

"Yes. He is." All of a sudden her heart seemed to split wide open, and she recognized the truth. She didn't just admire and care about Travis. She'd gone and fallen in love with him.

Chapter Six

She had to be careful, Annabel told herself a few days later at the farm. Very careful, so that Travis wouldn't guess her feelings for him. That would be awkward, to say the least. He was Luke's friend— her friend now, too. She couldn't do anything to ruin that. Maybe, eventually…

She resolutely turned her attention back to the children. She'd gathered them around Toby, the donkey.

"Now I want you to notice something." She looked around the circle of small faces. "See this marking on the donkey's back?" She traced the crossing stripes of paler fur. "What does it look like?"

"A cross," Charlie said, the words bursting out. "It looks like a cross, doesn't it, Miz Annabel?"

"That's right, Charlie. It looks like a cross."

"I was gonna say that." Kyle's face clouded. "I was gonna say it, but you butted in."

She put her hand on the boy's shoulder, touching him gently, and Kyle subsided. She couldn't look at him any longer without remembering Travis's suspicions, without worrying about it, praying she'd find a way to help.

"I could see that you knew it, too, Kyle. Why do you suppose the donkey has the mark of a cross on his back?"

No one spoke for a long moment. Then Mandie, leaning forward in her wheelchair, raised her hand. Annabel nodded at her. "Why do you think, Mandie?"

"Because a donkey carried Mary to Bethlehem?" She sounded uncertain.

"That's right." She traced the lines again. "I don't know if it's true or not, but that's what people have believed for a long time. That because a humble donkey carried the mother of Jesus, he received the mark of the cross on his back."

She sensed, without even looking his way, that Travis had joined the group. She was in a bad way, to be so aware of him that her skin seemed to tingle when he came near.

"And this donkey is going to be in the Nativity," Charlie said. "I am, too, and I'm gonna be a shepherd."

"Me, too," Kyle said quickly.

"That's right. And I hope all the rest of you will tell your parents about it so they can bring you to see it. I have some flyers, and I'll give you one before you leave today."

Several heads nodded, and she hoped the parents would follow through. It was far too easy to get caught up in all the other traditions that surrounded Christmas and forget the reason for the celebration.

"Toby is going to carry the girl who plays Mary in the Nativity, so I thought we might practice letting him give you a little ride today. We're not putting a saddle on him, just a blanket, so if that sounds scary, you don't have to do it."

"I want to." Mandie lifted her hand.

Her mother bent over her, looking distressed. "Mandie, I'm not sure that's a good idea."

"I'll hold her," Travis said quickly. "I can lift her off easily if need be."

Annabel looked at the child's mother, eyebrows lifting in a question. It must be a constant struggle with a child like Mandie to let her try the things she wanted to do.

She got a reluctant nod in return. "All right. Thank you." The thanks were directed toward Travis, who was already bending over Mandie.

"I want to do it next," Kyle insisted.

"No, me." Several voices spoke together.

"Everyone who wants to can have a turn as long as Toby agrees," she said solemnly. "Remember how hurt his back was when he first came here? We have to treat him gently. Don't forget that."

That seemed to satisfy them, and everyone watched while Travis settled Mandie gently on the donkey's back. He held her with both hands, and she gripped the donkey's neck. Glancing at Annabel, he gave a slight nod.

Make it a short ride. She could almost hear him say the words. They seemed to be on the same wavelength. She stepped forward, leading Toby with a hand on his halter.

Toby stepped out agreeably enough. Mandie was so light that he probably scarcely felt her weight on his back. They walked a dozen steps, then turned and came back without incident.

"Good job." Travis lifted Mandie and helped her down, and the gentleness in his face and his touch seemed to grab Annabel's heart and wring it. Yes, she had it bad.

Please, Lord… That prayer tapered off to nothing, because she didn't know what she wanted to pray. Please make him love me? No, she couldn't ask that.

One after another, the children who wanted to had their short rides. Annabel turned them over to one of her helpers as they finished, relieved that it had gone without incident.

"What do you think?" Travis asked when the

last child had finished. "Is Toby ready for his big role?"

"I hope so." She rubbed the donkey's nose, trying not to react to Travis's nearness. "We don't have much more time. I actually turned down the offer of a mule." She ran her fingers over the cross. "Somehow that just wouldn't seem right."

"Sentimental," Travis said, but there was teasing laughter in his voice. "I always knew you had a sentimental streak."

"Guilty," she admitted. "I know it's the message of the Nativity that's important, but I'd be disappointed if Mary didn't come in on a donkey. And if there weren't three wise men, even though I know the Bible doesn't actually mention three."

"It doesn't?" He started to lead Toby toward the barn, and she walked with him.

"Nope. Three gifts are mentioned but not three kings. And yet we're all so convinced that there were three that we'd be upset at any other suggestion."

"As you say, it's the message that's important. I remember…"

He let that trail off. Had he been about to confide something personal?

"What do you remember?"

He shrugged. "Just thinking of the first Christmas pageant I ever attended. I was staying with… with some friends, and they took me. I was totally awed."

It took an effort to keep her feelings from showing in her voice. "I hope that's what we can do for some child or adult with the Living Nativity. Show them the awesome nature of God's gift of the Christ."

He seemed touched, and he put his hand over hers. "I hope so, too."

Maybe someday. She found herself thinking that again. Maybe someday Travis would look at her and see love.

The afternoon slipped away, her time working with the children too short, as always. Annabel couldn't help wishing these sessions were longer. They were doing good work with the children; she was convinced of that. It was just sometimes tough to show quantifiable results.

She'd just supervised the pickup of the youngest children. She headed back to the barn, intent on making sure that the older kids had done the assigned cleanup work before their van arrived.

An angry shout alerted her, and she headed for the barn at a run, reaching it in time to see Travis pulling Kyle and Charlie apart. Again.

Her heart sank. She'd thought Kyle's behavior had begun to improve. It looked as if she'd been wrong. What was she going to do? She couldn't have him here with the other children if he continued to start fights.

"What happened?" She pulled Charlie to her side,

since Travis still had his hand on Kyle's shoulder. "I can't believe you two are fighting again."

"Not my fault." Charlie's words seemed to wobble on the edge of tears. "I didn't mean to push Kyle. It was an accident, honest. I'm sorry."

"Okay, Charlie." She ruffled his hair. "Why don't you run over to the kitchen and get a drink of water? The van will be here soon."

He nodded, sniffling a little, and darted out of the barn.

Annabel turned to Kyle, sending up a fervent prayer for guidance. "Kyle, what's going on?"

Kyle's face was set in angry lines. "He pushed me."

She knelt in front of him, meeting his eyes. "You heard what Charlie said. He didn't mean to do it. It was an accident. Do you think he was lying?"

"Maybe." His bottom lip shoved out. "I don't know. Guess not."

"Then why…"

"I think I know why." Travis's voice was rough with emotion. Hands on Kyle's shoulders, he turned the boy to face him. "You feel mad inside all the time. You want to hit before somebody hits you."

"Travis." She put a warning in her voice, but he didn't even glance at her.

Kyle stared at the floor. "Maybe."

"Hitting isn't right," Travis said. "Especially not

when somebody hurts an animal, like Toby. Or a kid, like you."

"Travis, don't." Alarm swept through her.

"That's it, isn't it?" Travis didn't seem to hear her. "Your dad hits you, doesn't he, Kyle? Tell me."

Kyle stared at him, eyes wide. Then he spun away from Travis's grip. "No!" he shouted. "Don't you say that! Don't you ever say that!"

He ran from the barn and kept on running toward the waiting van.

For a moment, Annabel slumped back on her heels, feeling as if someone had hit her. Then anger propelled her to her feet.

"How could you do that? You didn't have the right to interfere in this. I told you Pastor Tim was handling it."

Travis's hands clenched into fists. His face tightened into a forbidding mask. "I had to."

"No, you didn't have to." Frustration battled pain as she tried to think of all the things that could happen as a result of Travis's words. "Don't you understand what you've done?"

"I've given that kid a chance—"

"He denied it. You heard him. And if he tells his parents, they'll pull him out of the program, and any chance I have of helping him will be gone. They'll probably blame Pastor Tim, as well. And if they complain to my board—" she stopped for a moment, not wanting to even consider that "—I could lose my backing. I could lose my whole program because of this."

It was as if he couldn't absorb what she was saying to him. "I'm right about Kyle. I know I'm right."

She threw up her hands. "How?" she demanded. "How do you know that you're right, Travis?"

Life seemed to come back into the bleakness of his face. His mouth twisted in pain. "Because it happened to me, okay? I know because I lived it. My father beat me every day of my life, until the law finally took me away from him. I know the signs. I know."

Shock and pain fought for control of her heart. "Travis, I…I don't know what to say." She reached toward him. "I…"

"Don't say anything." He ground the words out. "Don't. I can't talk about it."

And like Kyle, he turned and left her there.

Travis took the chair Pastor Tim indicated in his study. He sat stiffly on the edge of the chair, feeling as if his hands were too big and his body too awkward. Annabel had nodded when he came into the room, her lips curving in a stilted smile.

Well, he couldn't be surprised at that. She hadn't spoken to him since that explosion at her barn the previous day. It had been Pastor Tim who'd called, asking him to come in to discuss Kyle's situation.

He'd had to agree. No way out of it. He'd done this

thing, and while he still felt that someone had had to confront Kyle, he'd begun to wonder if he'd been the right one to do it.

Or to do it the way he had. His stomach twisted at the thought of Annabel's words, at the pain in her face. He hadn't thought about her. He'd only known that the kid was a mirror, showing him his own face at that age. And he'd had to break through that.

"Well, now." Pastor Tim looked from one to the other. "I thought it best if we talk this through together before we decide what the next step is."

Annabel's face was white. "Is there any choice? Don't I have to go to Kyle's parents?"

Travis swallowed hard. He'd put that look on her face. This was his responsibility.

"That wouldn't be right," he said, looking at the wall of books behind Pastor Tim's desk because it hurt too much to look at Annabel. "I'm the one who spoke to Kyle. Annabel tried to stop me. I'm the one who is responsible, not her."

"It's my program." Her voice was firm. "I'm responsible for everything that happens there."

Pastor Tim cleared his throat, bringing their attention to him. "Let's not be hasty. We're here to talk about the possibilities, not to lay or accept blame."

"I don't want Annabel hurt by something I did."

Pastor Tim focused on Travis's face, but Travis had the feeling the man looked into his very soul.

It was an uncomfortable sensation. It took an effort not to turn away from that probing gaze.

"I understand," the pastor said. "Now, let's look at what can happen. If Kyle tells his parents, I think we can expect them to react strongly."

"That's putting it mildly. I've been jumping every time the phone rings, sure they'll be calling." Annabel's hands twisted together in her lap, a sign of distress he'd learned to recognize.

"They haven't?" Pastor Tim asked.

"No. Not yet."

"If they do, I would imagine they'll be angry. I don't want you to deal with that alone, Annabel. If they contact you, you should insist that they meet with the two of us to discuss this."

For a moment, Annabel looked as if she'd argue the point, but then she nodded, silently agreeing with the pastor. "They'll be angry," she said. "I can't blame them for that. Maybe angry enough to go to the board."

"We'll cross that bridge when we get to it," Pastor Tim said. "You know I'll support you with the board, don't you?"

She nodded. "Thank you," she murmured.

Travis couldn't stand it any longer. "You have to let me talk to them, if it comes to that. They can't dismiss all the good Annabel does with those kids because I felt I had to confront Kyle."

Pastor Tim studied him. Had Annabel told

him what he'd revealed about his childhood? His face burned at the thought. He didn't tell people. He'd wiped that part of his life out. But he'd told Annabel.

"As I said, let's not leap ahead of ourselves. Now, I've been giving this a lot of thought since Annabel called me yesterday. And I've been giving it a lot of time in prayer." He closed his eyes for a moment, as if he still prayed. "It seems to me that the answer I'm getting is clear. Wait."

"Wait?" Annabel's voice expressed dismay. "Pastor, I'd rather just get this over with. I can't—"

She stopped when he raised his hand. His lips curved in a faint smile.

"I know. That's my reaction, too. Rush in and try to make it better. I have to admit that I've been arguing with God about this."

"Well, then…" She let that taper off.

"If we rush in, we may precipitate something. It may be that God has something else in mind. Sometimes the hardest thing we can do is wait for Him."

The words seemed to sink into Travis's heart, setting up an echo that reverberated through him. "I didn't wait. That hasn't turned out very well."

"We don't know that yet," Pastor Tim said. "We're assuming Kyle will tell his parents, and then they'll react. But what if he doesn't?"

Annabel stared at him, forehead crinkled. "I don't

understand. If he doesn't, don't we have a duty to tell them?"

"We have a duty to do what's best for that boy. If Kyle doesn't tell his parents, I'm beginning to think that in itself may tell us something." He paused, clasping his hands on the surface of the desk. "I think it might tell us that Travis's suspicions are correct."

Silence greeted his words. Travis didn't know about Annabel, but he'd been stunned into silence. He had never thought of that, but the more he looked at it, the surer he became. Pastor Tim was right. The natural thing to do was for Kyle to run to his parents with Travis's accusation. If he didn't, it had to mean something.

"I'm assuming by your silence that you agree—or at least that you'll go along with me on this." Pastor Tim looked at Annabel.

After a long moment, she nodded. "I'll follow your lead. But if we don't hear any response from them, then what will we do?"

"I don't know. It may be that we'll have to consult Children's Services. Or we may find that Travis's words will open Kyle to talk to us. Either way, we'll find our way through this, with God's help. Agreed?"

Travis waited for Annabel.

"Agreed," she said.

Pastor Tim looked at him, and he nodded.

"Let's pray together." Pastor Tim held out his hands to them.

Travis took the pastor's extended hand and then reached out tentatively to Annabel. She put her hand in his.

"Gracious Lord, we know that You see all of Your children as precious. We come to You agreeing in prayer for Kyle, knowing that You want nothing but good for him. We ask that we might be Your humble instruments to do Your will in Kyle's life."

Travis's breath caught in his throat. His heart hurt, as if something real and physical affected it as a result of the pastor's prayer.

"Use us as You will, dear Father. We know that You have work for us to do in this world, and we want only to serve You. In Jesus's precious name we pray. Amen."

"Amen," Annabel said softly.

He wanted to do the same, but he'd choke if he tried to speak. Something was happening to him. He didn't know what it was, but he knew it was changing him forever.

Chapter Seven

Two days had gone by, and nothing had happened. Travis had been trying to steer clear of Annabel, figuring that was the least he could do for her. But Miz Callie dropped by the house, determined that he go with her to the dress rehearsal for the Living Nativity. So here he was, suiting his long strides to the elderly woman's steps as they walked down the block toward the church.

"…know how much help you've been to Annabel with getting the animals ready for this." Miz Callie looked up at him with that pert, birdlike gaze. "I'm sure she'll need all the helping hands she can get tonight."

"I'm glad to help." Except that according to Annabel, his help might well have wrecked her program. Had Kyle said anything to his parents? He didn't know, and if Annabel did, she hadn't confided in him.

Would she have talked to her grandmother? From what he could see, they were very close, but surely Miz Callie wouldn't be acting so friendly toward him if Annabel had told her what he'd done.

"This event means so much to Annabel." Miz Callie's steps slowed a bit. Maybe he'd been walking too fast for her. "I do believe she's been tryin' to find a way to repay Pastor Tim for helping her through a bad time a couple of years ago." Again, that gaze was fixed on him. "Did Luke tell you about the wedding?"

"Not Luke. Annabel mentioned it."

"She did?" Miz Callie's expression seemed to speculate on that.

"Not much," he said hurriedly. "Just that she was supposed to be married at Christmastime, and the guy broke it off."

"Christmas Eve. That's when the wedding was to be. And the night before, after the rehearsal, he told her he wasn't ready to get married."

"I'm sorry." The words seemed inadequate.

"Mind now, I never did think that Foster Sharrow was the right man for her at all. But being left that way really shook Annabel. It seemed to drive her right into her shell." Miz Callie put her hand on his arm, halting him as they neared the churchyard. "I'm glad you're here this Christmas, Travis. Seems to me it's been good for her to be busy with entertaining you. Keeps her from brooding on the past." She shook her head. "The past is for learning from, not for living in. But I guess every generation has to find that out for themselves."

Before he could find a response to that, she'd moved briskly on toward the makeshift stable.

He followed her, struggling with himself. Annabel's good deed in entertaining him this Christmas was in danger of costing her the thing she valued most in the world. If Kyle had complained about him—

Well, whether the boy had or not, he'd handled it badly. He couldn't seem to forget the pastor's words about waiting for God. If God was indeed using them as His tools—

He backed away from that thought. If God was looking for someone to accomplish things, He surely wouldn't pick Travis McCall.

Annabel was a far more likely choice. A cold hand seemed to grip his heart. Annabel might not want to have anything to do with him, but at least he had to tell her how sorry he was that she was hurt by what he'd done.

He drew closer, scanning the crowd. Kids in costumes scurried around, and a choir was rehearsing off to one side. Hugh seemed to be testing the stability of the stable they'd worked on together a few days ago.

He spotted Kyle, tussling with a couple of other

boys. He was bundled up to the neck in a shepherd's robe. If there were any bruises on Kyle, no one would see them in that outfit.

An outraged bray helped him locate Annabel. She'd pulled the truck and trailer into the side street, and Toby seemed no more eager to get off the trailer than he had been to get on that first time Travis had met Annabel. Travis trotted across the lawn.

He seized the opposite side of the halter and helped Annabel ease Toby down the ramp. She looked flushed and flustered, and for a moment when she glanced at him across the donkey's back, her eyes were laughing again.

"Didn't we do this once before?" he asked.

She nodded, seemed about to speak, but then the barriers went up again and she froze.

He reached across Toby's back to catch her arm. "Wait, Annabel. Just let me say one thing. I'm sorry. I was wrong. If I can do anything to make it right, I will."

She took a deep breath. Some of the tension seemed to ease out of her face. "So far it looks as if Kyle hasn't said anything to his parents." She hesitated and then managed a tentative smile. "I understand why it happened, Travis."

She looked as if she'd say more, but Pastor Tim started calling her name. She spun away from Travis, handing him the donkey's lead line. "Hold him for a minute, will you? I've got to see what's going on."

She hurried away to be met by three or four people who all seemed to have questions for her, to say nothing of the kids who gathered around when they saw her. Annabel had a smile and a greeting for each of them, her hand resting lightly on one child's shoulder while she hugged another and explained something to one of the adults.

He patted the donkey absently, trying to get rid of the feeling that someone was trampling on his heart. But he couldn't. He cared for Annabel—cared big time. And he didn't know what he was going to do about it.

Annabel's mind seemed to split into two competing halves as the rehearsal straggled onward, part of her attention focused on the rehearsal, but the rest was on the issue with Kyle. To say nothing of her heart, aching for Travis.

Enough, she scolded herself. Focus.

Amanda was corralling the children, sorting them into groups according to their roles. Annabel couldn't help smiling. Now that she was engaged, Amanda had developed an increased interest in children, maybe looking ahead to the family she and Ross would have one day.

She joined Sam, who had the animals in a makeshift pen, ready to go.

"I still say we shoulda brought some chickens,"

Sam said. "Stands to reason they'd have had chickens, don't you think?"

"The last thing we need is to try and hang on to a bunch of chickens in this situation," she said. "Watch it, you're about to lose a sheep."

Sam caught the ewe. Miz Callie grasped a small angel whose efforts to pet the sheep had startled it.

"Sorry about that." She turned the child around and gave her a gentle shove. "You get on over with the other angels, y'heah?"

"Yes, ma'am, Miz Callie. Can I pet the sheep after?"

"We'll see. If Annabel says it's okay. Go on now."

The angel departed, wings askew, with a wistful look at the sheep.

"Gracious, those children are a handful," Miz Callie said. "They're already excited enough about Christmas, and you add in some real animals and they're about fit to burst. Looks like Travis isn't quite ready to hand the donkey over to that young Joseph."

"Not until the last possible moment, I hope," Annabel said.

She still didn't have complete confidence in Toby. She let her gaze linger on Travis. He had a grip on the donkey's halter while he gave some quiet directions to the young teenager who was dressed as Joseph.

Just looking at him made her heart clutch, knowing

the pain that lurked behind his stoic facade. What he'd told her about his childhood was bad enough, and she didn't doubt that there was plenty he hadn't said.

The wonder was that he'd stuck around the farm at all once he'd learned that some of her kids were abuse victims. It had taken courage to hang in there, but Travis had plenty of that.

Angry as she'd been over his action in questioning Kyle, she understood why he'd done it. Looking at the boy was like looking at himself.

"There, now." Miz Callie rejoined her. "All the angels are in their places."

"For the moment," Annabel said.

The plan was to have the participants arrive at the stable as the choir sang and then to stay in their positions for the better part of an hour, while people drove or walked past.

"I remember being an angel. The halo itched something fierce, and it was all I could do to stay still."

"You did it, though." Miz Callie had a reminiscent smile. "I remember one year when it seemed half the cast was made up of Bodines. Then the boys got big enough to rebel at the idea of wearing costumes."

"I think they secretly enjoyed it, but they'd never admit that."

The choir began to sing. It was time for Mary

and Joseph to arrive on the scene. She held her breath and Joseph started forward, holding the lead rope…a real rope, instead of the synthetic lead lines she normally used.

Toby walked forward obediently for several paces. Then, apparently seeing something that interested him, he veered off to the right, taking Joseph and Mary with him.

Annabel started toward them but stopped before she'd gone more than a few steps. Travis was there already, getting Toby back on course, showing the boy how to keep the donkey headed in the right direction.

She let out a breath of relief. Miz Callie nodded approvingly.

"That Travis is a man a person can depend on," she said. "Guess you've already found that out, since you told him about Foster."

"How do you know that?" she demanded. Really, Miz Callie had an uncanny knack for knowing what her family was up to.

"Well, I thought maybe Luke had told him, but he said you did."

Which still didn't explain why the subject had come up to begin with. "You're not trying to match-make, are you? Because it's not going to work."

Miz Callie just smiled.

The shepherds were headed toward the stable with

their sheep, and Annabel watched Kyle. His face was intent and serious but not sullen or rebellious.

Surely Travis was mistaken about the boy. She went over the arguments again in her mind, unable to let it go. Travis could be wrong. But if he wasn't…

The three kings set off toward the stable, leading the llama who was standing in for a camel. All went well until they reached the manger, where the kings went down on their knees to worship the Baby Jesus. The llama, suddenly presented with a gold foil crown right in front of his nose, decided to see if it was something edible, which naturally had all the kids dissolving in laughter and shouting except for the unfortunate king.

Darting forward, Annabel grabbed the llama and rescued the crown.

"There, good as new." She handed it back. "Everything's fine now."

"Except for the donkey," Amanda pointed out. "He seems to have his nose in the manger."

"Remind me again why I got involved in this?" she muttered. She grabbed Toby. Catching sight of Kyle and Charlie, she beckoned to them.

"Listen, you two know Toby. How about if you take charge of him once you get up here, okay? Can I count on you?"

"Yes, ma'am." Kyle straightened. "We can handle him."

"Good." She smiled at him. "Tomorrow night I'll

have a little bag of oats for you, and you can feed him if he gets fidgety, okay?"

"We'll do it," Charlie assured her. "Leave it to us."

"Good job." She stepped back out of the scene, still smiling. Travis was wrong about Kyle, she told herself again. He had to be.

"Okay, everyone, that's perfect," Amanda said. "Now freeze like that." She glanced at Annabel. "What's the old saying? A bad dress rehearsal means a good performance? I sure hope that's right."

"It'll be fine," Annabel assured her. "And if it's not perfect, people will love it anyway."

"True enough. Okay, everyone." Annabel raised her voice. "That's it for now. Remember to be on time tomorrow, and don't forget your costume."

The manger scene dissolved suddenly, and for the next few minutes, Annabel, along with Travis and Sam, was completely occupied in collecting the animals. She was vaguely aware of parents arriving to pick up children, Amanda collecting props and Miz Callie comforting an angel who was crying, it seemed, over a broken wing.

"We got some oats at home." Charlie said, turning up at her side with Kyle. "You want us each to bring some in our pockets?"

"That's okay." She smiled at them, relieved to see that they seemed to have turned into the best of friends. "I'll take care of that. I don't want you raiding the breakfast cereal."

"My mamma wouldn't mind," Charlie said earnestly. "She'll be here to get me in a minute, so I can ask her."

Kyle nodded, his eyes bright with enthusiasm. "We can…"

"Kyle, there you are." Kyle's father spoke. Kyle's mother put her hand on his shoulder. And Annabel felt as if someone had punched her right in the heart.

Kyle's face changed. In an instant, he was transformed from a smiling, normal kid to a sullen, angry stranger. And behind the anger, she saw it.

Fear. Kyle was afraid.

Her heart twisted, forming a wordless prayer. Kyle was afraid. Travis was right.

An accusation of abuse, once made, could shatter lives for good. True or false, it was such a serious thing that the burden of it seemed to weigh on Annabel's shoulders, dragging them down.

She sat at the kitchen table at the farm the evening after the dress rehearsal. Tomorrow would be the real thing, and as worrisome as that was, it didn't hold a candle to her fears for the situation with Kyle.

The report on her laptop was for the board that supported her work at the farm. Without their backing, there would be no children's program. If she accused Kyle's parents of abuse without proof, her work would end, and all the good she'd done would come to nothing. Pastor Tim had said to wait, but she was discovering just how hard that was.

She leaned back in the chair, the silence pressing on her. It was nearly dark out, and the single Christmas candle in each window reflected gold against the panes.

The glass formed a mirror, showing her the interior of the cozy farmhouse kitchen with its brick walls and exposed beams. The herbs she'd cut dried in bunches hung from the beams, their faint aroma filling the air.

She could see herself in the reflection, too, and the troubled expression she wore as she tried to find an answer.

Tried to figure it out for herself, she realized. She was forgetting to turn to the One she should rely on.

She clasped her hands, bowing her head. Trying to still the furious clamor of her thoughts.

Dear Father, thank You for bringing Kyle into my life. I want to help him, and I'm not sure what to do. I know that You care for Kyle in a way that is impossible for me, so I'm asking for Your guidance. If I'm meant to help Kyle, please show me the way and give me the courage to take it. In Jesus' name, Amen.

She sat for another moment, head bowed against her hands. Then she stood. No answer flooded her mind, but she had a sense of peace. The answer would come. She just had to recognize it.

She moved to the sink, reaching for a glass, and looked out the window, seeing past the reflection to what lay outside. She froze, frowning. A faint light came from the barn.

It could be Sam, she supposed, but the lights were on in his apartment above the garage. Then she recognized the car that was parked at the edge of the lane—Travis's car. He'd left hours ago. Obviously, he'd returned.

She went quickly out the back door, grabbing her denim jacket from the hook. Why was Travis here? More to the point, why hadn't he told her he was back?

She crossed the grass to the barn and slipped in the door that stood ajar. Her breath caught.

For just a moment it was like stepping back in time to that stable in Bethlehem. The scent of hay and animals, the soft sounds they made moving in the stalls—those things hadn't changed in thousands of years, and it overwhelmed her. She had to blink back tears. This was what they tried to do for others with the Living Nativity.

Travis stood in a circle of light cast by the lantern that hung from a post. He faced Toby, who watched him with wary eyes. Deliberately, Travis put the lead line on the floor in front of Toby's front hooves.

"Stand," he said, palm out, and took a step back.

Toby moved toward him.

"No." Travis's voice was firm. He took the halter and nudged the donkey back to his previous position. "Stand," he said again, palm out.

This time Toby let him get several steps away, standing motionless.

"Good boy." Travis returned quickly, pulling a carrot from his pocket and feeding it to Toby as he stroked the furry neck. "Good boy. Good Toby."

Travis was going to all the trouble of teaching the donkey to ground tie just so the Nativity would be a success. Her heart swelled with love and admiration.

She wasn't the only one who admired Travis. Despite his reaction to Travis's questioning, Kyle clearly did, as well. Each day the bond between them seemed to grow stronger.

The idea slid into her mind, so natural it was as if she'd thought it all along. If Travis were to tell Kyle his own story—

She must have moved or made some sound. Travis turned and saw her.

She went toward him quickly. "I can't believe it. You actually taught Toby to ground tie."

"Well, let's say I'm trying." After the initial

surprise at seeing her, Travis seemed to relax. "He's not the most teachable critter in the world, but he's making progress. I figured it might help his performance a bit."

"I'm sure of it." She rubbed the donkey's face. Her fingers brushed Travis's, and awareness of him went shimmering through her.

He clasped her hand, fingers curling around hers. "Annabel." He said her name softly. "I've been trying to do what we agreed—to stay friends, nothing more." He shook his head slightly. His dark gaze focused on her face, and her skin seemed to warm where it touched. "I can't."

He hesitated a moment, as if waiting for her to say something or pull away. She didn't.

He raised his hand to her face, tilting it toward his. His lips neared, touched, clung. Her heart pounded until she thought it would leap from her body. She put her palm on his chest, and his own heart seemed to beat in rhythm with hers. The moment stretched out, timeless.

Toby's head moved, jolting them. They came apart, Annabel's breath catching on a gasp.

Travis gave a low chuckle. "Guess Toby doesn't approve."

"He just wants some attention, that's all." She rubbed the donkey's muzzle, trying to get control of the emotions that rampaged through her. She ought to be thanking Toby. Without his interruption, she might have completely lost her ability to think rationally at all.

Maybe she already had, where Travis was concerned. She took a shaky breath. She couldn't do this. She had to find the courage to talk to him about Kyle. To say the thing she knew he didn't want to hear.

"Travis, I…I have to ask you something. About Kyle. I want you to talk to him."

His expression changed indefinably. "We agreed to wait, remember. Anyway, I thought you didn't want me to talk to him at all."

"Maybe I was wrong." *Please, Lord, guide my words.* "I've seen how Kyle looks at you. He admires you."

He shook his head, eyes questioning. "I don't think—"

"I want you to tell Kyle your story." She rushed the words, because otherwise she might not be able to get them out. "If you do, if he understands what you went through, it could give him the courage to tell the truth."

He didn't move. Maybe he couldn't. Suddenly, nothing seemed alive about him but the torment in his eyes.

"Don't ask that." He thrust her hands away from him in a gesture so abrupt that Toby jerked back.

"I don't want to." Her voice thickened with tears. "I know it's painful. But if Kyle heard it—"

He grew a ragged breath. "I'd do anything to help him. To help you."

"Then—"

His face twisted. "But that's the one thing I can't do. Don't you understand? I can't."

He turned and walked out.

Chapter Eight

"Here you go, little guy." Travis nudged the straying sheep back into the makeshift pen on the church lawn. "You don't want to go wandering off."

But he did. He'd give a lot to be anywhere but here at the moment.

"He don't...doesn't...know when he's well off," Sam said, patting the small Nubian goat.

Travis nodded, but his mind wasn't on the goat. It was on Annabel.

Thinking about her was just asking for pain. Still, he couldn't seem to quit. The chasm between them was so wide and deep that it couldn't be crossed.

Annabel wanted him to do the one thing he couldn't do. It had been hard enough to give even Annabel that glimpse into his past. To tell the story to someone else—to a child, no less, was impossible.

Annabel ought to know. He stopped that line of thought, his jaw clenching. He couldn't blame this on

Annabel. It was his choice. He'd survived by clamping a tight lid on his past and never letting it out.

That was his way. He couldn't put that onto anyone else.

Sam nudged him. "Looks like they're almost ready to start. You think that donkey's gonna behave?"

"He'd better, for Annabel's sake."

"Yeah."

He saw, on Sam's face, the same look that was probably on his. The longing to have all this go well because it was what Annabel wanted.

"You think a lot of her, don't you?"

"Miz Annabel? She's the best. If it wasn't for her, I dunno what would have happened to me."

Travis felt a flicker of shame that it had never occurred to him to wonder about the boy. "She gave you a job," he said.

"More'n that." He gave Travis a look that seemed to measure his interest. "See, my mamma used to work for Miz Callie, when she lived at the house in Charleston. After Mamma died—" pain flickered in the boy's dark eyes. "—things got bad with my daddy. Quick with his fists and his belt, he was."

The words were like a blow, knocking a hole in his heart. Sam was looking at him. He had to say something.

"I'm sorry. I didn't know." Why hadn't Annabel told him? Maybe because she'd seen his reaction to Kyle.

"Miz Callie, she's a special lady. Stood up to my daddy, got me out of there. And Miz Annabel gave me a job and a place to live." He grinned. "Now she's nagged me into getting my GED. Says I need to do something with my life. I tell you, you might as well give in if Miz Annabel wants you to do something."

The words echoed uncomfortably. "So what do you want to do with your life?"

Sam shrugged. "I'd rather work with the animals than anything. Miz Annabel says there's no reason I can't aim high. Be a vet, maybe." He shrugged, his gaze slipping away. "Maybe that's aimin' too high."

Travis put his hand on the boy's shoulder. "Miz Annabel's right. You'll never know unless you try."

He'd never fancied himself good at giving advice, but Sam seemed to take heart at his words. The boy smiled, standing a little straighter.

"Yeah. Maybe so."

The choir began to sing. "O Come, All Ye Faithful" rang out, silencing the murmurs of the crowd, calling them to worship, it seemed.

His gaze sought out Annabel. She stood with Toby and the kids playing Mary and Joseph, waiting for their moment. Her hand rested on the donkey's neck, and she was saying something softly to the kids.

Encouragement, probably. That was Annabel.

Encouraging, warm, giving. A woman in a million. He loved her.

The thought hit him with the impact of a two-ton truck. He loved her. He'd put an impossible barrier between them, but he loved her.

The choir switched to the hymn that was the signal for Mary and Joseph's arrival—"Once in Royal David's City." He held his breath as Joseph took the rope and led the donkey forward. And then he let the breath out in a sigh of relief. Toby plodded along as patiently as if he really did carry the mother of Jesus on his back.

The pageant moved forward. That sense of peace and purpose that affected the little donkey must be contagious. The animals, the children, the music— everything came together as if inspired. Maybe it was.

For God so loved the world... The spoken words set up an echo in his heart, reverberating until it seemed his whole body felt them.

His mind spun with confusion. Pain. How could he let himself believe in a Father who loved him? How could he not?

He couldn't take it. He couldn't. He slipped away into the silent night.

From where she stood, to the side of the stable ready to intervene in case of problems, Annabel had a good view of the crowd. She could see the effect on them—the smiles and the tears. And she could see Travis leave.

She pressed her lips together. She would not let them tremble. As for the tears in her eyes—well, plenty of people had those. No one would know if she wept for what she had lost.

An arm went around her, and she turned to find her grandmother next to her. "It's beautiful," Miz Callie murmured, and tears filled her eyes, too. "And the animals are perfect."

"So far." She glanced at her watch. "They're supposed to remain in position for the next hour, so that people driving by can see them. That might be asking a lot of kids and animals."

"They'll be fine." There was no doubt in Miz Callie's voice. "It's as if they all realize that this is something special. Sacred."

She nodded. "That was what I thought when Toby walked on. It was as if he really understood who he was supposed to be carrying."

"Maybe the animals know more than we think," Miz Callie said. "After all, God chose them to be part of that first Christmas."

She clasped her grandmother's hand. They stood silently for a few minutes, watching the scene, listening to the music.

Annabel let out her breath in a sigh. "You know how we sometimes use Christmas as a measuring stick? We say, 'That was a great or happy Christmas,' or whatever?"

Miz Callie nodded. "Foolish, isn't it?"

"That's not what Christmas is, is it?"

"No." Her grandmother's voice was soft. "Christmas is holy and humble and a time for astonished joy that God loves us so much. It can't be measured in human terms."

Annabel nodded, her throat too tight to speak. And when her tears spilled over, she knew they were for the right reason. For the incredible gift that was Christmas, not for her own heartache.

Miz Callie squeezed her hand. "You and Amanda did a wonderful job. I'd best find her and tell her so, too."

She moved off, and Annabel stood where she was, gazing at the scene, thinking over the events of the past weeks. She seemed to see everything more clearly now.

She had taken on entertaining Travis for motives that were at least partly selfish. Oh, she'd done it because he was her brother's friend, of course. But she'd also thought it would distract her from memories of the past.

It had worked too well, hadn't it? Knowing Travis, caring about him, had made her realize just how flimsy her relationship with Foster had been.

She thought of that now with astonishment. She had wasted two years grieving over a man who wasn't worth a second thought. And now that she'd found someone who was, she'd lost him.

It hurt. It would go on hurting. But through the pain the healing power of Christmas flowed, and she knew she was not alone.

"Where is he?"

The shrill voice, loud in Annabel's ear, startled her. Startled Toby, too, and he jerked back against the lead line.

Annabel soothed him with a pat and a gentle word and then turned to the woman who'd spoken. "Mrs. Morrison." She recognized Kyle's mother, and her stomach gave an uncomfortable lurch. "Is something wrong?"

"Where is Kyle?" The woman grabbed her arm and gave it a shake. "Where is he?"

Dread pooled in her chest. "What do you mean? He was here a few minutes ago." She glanced across the area. Quite a few people lingered, either helping with the cleanup or chatting.

"Judith, calm down." Don Morrison appeared at his wife's side, closely followed by Pastor Tim and Amanda. "I'm sure Kyle is here somewhere. We weren't more than a few minutes late." He glanced at Pastor Tim with a look of apology. "Sorry to miss it, Pastor. I've been away on business overnight, and Judith came to the airport to pick me up. We thought we'd get here in time to see some of the program, but my flight was a bit late."

"Of course." Pastor Tim was clearly not interested in why Kyle's parents arrived late. "Now, when did each of you last see Kyle?"

Amanda's brow wrinkled. "He was on stage until the very end, when I brought the kids off. They were milling around a bit—supposed to be taking off their costumes, but there was a certain amount of horse-play going on."

"Only natural when they'd been still so long," Pastor Tim said, his voice calm and soothing. "Anyone else see him?"

"He brought the donkey over." Annabel gestured with the lead line, as if that would help. Her mind seemed numb. What had happened to him? "I asked if he wanted to help load the animals, but he said he had to go."

Sam took the lead rope. "That's right. I heard him. Usually he wants to help but not tonight."

She nodded, trying to keep her expression calm even as her mind raced and her stomach tumbled. "You go on with the loading, will you, Sam? Just check in and around the truck and trailer as you do."

"Sure thing, Miz Annabel." Sam clucked to Toby and led him away.

"He was supposed to wait here for us." Judith Morrison's voice trembled, and there was an edge to it which suggested hysteria wasn't too far off.

Her husband put his hand on her shoulder. "Take it easy, honey."

Annabel looked from his face to hers. Was what Travis believed true? If Don Morrison did beat his son, had Kyle disappeared because his father was coming back tonight?

"I think we need to talk to the kids who are still here before we do anything else." Pastor Tim took control with calm assurance. "Amanda, will you and Annabel round them up? I'll get a few people started searching the church. He might easily have gone inside."

Annabel exchanged glances with Amanda, knowing they were both thinking the same thing. Where was the boy? Was he safe?

"I'll take this side." Amanda gestured to the area of church lawn to the right of the sidewalk. "You take the other. Tell them to gather in front of the stable."

Annabel nodded, used to Amanda taking the lead. After all, she'd been doing that since they were born. She hurried across the lawn, catching parents and children as she went and sending them back to the stable, not pausing to explain.

In a few minutes, they'd collected everyone who was still on the premises. Some would have left as soon as the pageant was over. Amanda would have a list. They could start calling.

Pastor Tim raised his hands for quiet. "Sorry to keep y'all, but we need to locate Kyle Morrison. He was supposed to wait for his parents, but he's not here. Has anyone seen him since the end of the program?"

Annabel's hands clenched into fists. Pastor Tim was deliberate. Better than rushing off in all directions at once. Better than alarming everyone. But she wanted to do something—anything.

A few people raised their hands at the pastor's question. "We'll want to talk to each of you," he said. "Everyone else can go on home, if you want."

One of the deacons exchanged glances with his wife. "We'll stay and help look for the boy," he said.

Other heads nodded. Within minutes, small groups started searching the church, the education building and the grounds.

Annabel surveyed the small group, which had admitted seeing Kyle after the program ended. Her gaze lingered on Charlie. He looked down, intent on digging a hole in the turf with his toe.

She put a gentle hand on his shoulder and squatted down. "Charlie, did Kyle say anything to you tonight?"

He shrugged, not meeting her eyes. "I dunno."

She touched his chin, urging his face up, and gave

him what she hoped was a reassuring smile. "Come on, Charlie. Nobody's mad at you. But we need to find Kyle. He could get hurt out there by himself at night." A shiver went through her at the truth of the words.

Please, God, keep him safe.

Charlie's lips trembled, and he pressed them together. Then he nodded. "Okay. He said as how he wasn't goin' home tonight." He looked at her, eyes wide, and she thought he was telling the truth. "That's all I know, honest, Miz Annabel. I didn't see him go."

She gave the boy a quick hug. "Okay, Charlie. It's not your fault."

"He should have told us that right away." Judith Morrison dashed tears away with a quick gesture. "We have to find Kyle. We have to!"

"We will," Pastor Tim said. "The police—"

Judith shook her head. "No. Not the police. They'd scare him. Can't we find him ourselves?"

"When he ran away before, we found him at a friend's house." Don Morrison's voice was tight with strain. "Let's make some calls."

Annabel tugged on Pastor Tim's arm, drawing him a little aside. "I think the police should be called." She said the words quietly, not eager to get into open conflict with the Morrisons. "No matter why Kyle ran away, this is getting too serious." Surely, if the police became involved, the truth would come out.

"I agree," he said. "If the parents don't locate him with any of his friends, I'll take the responsibility on myself to call the police." He paused, looking at her searchingly. "Do you think he could be trying to go to the farm? It's obvious he loves the place."

"I don't know how he'd get there, but it's worth trying." She dug in her bag for her keys. "I'll go check. I have my cell phone with me. Call me if you learn anything."

"Right. Don't worry too much." He smiled faintly. "Praying is much more useful."

"I know." Keys gripped in her hands, she set off toward her car at a run. If there was any chance Kyle had gone to the farm, she'd find him. And she'd get the truth out of him, one way or another. This situation couldn't go on.

She was pulling out of the lot when she realized there was one other place Kyle might have gone, to one other person he seemed to trust—Travis. He could have gone to Travis.

Chapter Nine

Travis stopped halfway down the stairs at the Bodine house when the front door burst open. Annabel shot into the hallway. One look at her white, strained face told him that something was very wrong.

He bolted down the steps, conscious only of the need to reach her, and grasped her arms.

"What is it? Are you hurt?" The need to take care of her overwhelmed him like a giant wave at sea, crashing through all his barriers.

"It's Kyle." She gasped out the words, her voice shaking. Her fingers closed over his forearms. She took a breath. "He's not here?" Her gaze searched his face. "I thought he might come to you."

"I haven't seen him since the pageant." He clasped her hands in both of his. "What's happened? Did he run away again?"

She nodded, seeming to regain her composure with each passing second. "I...I'm sorry if I startled you. I just felt so panicky all of a sudden." She drew her hands away. "We'd finished, and we were clearing up when Kyle's parents came for him. He wasn't there."

"They hadn't come to the Nativity?" The memory of the emotions that had flooded him came back, and he set it aside. Right now, he had to concentrate on the boy.

"Apparently, Mr. Morrison had been away on business, and his wife went to the airport to pick him up. They didn't get there until it was over." Her eyes darkened. "And Kyle was gone."

"Didn't anyone see—"

"He apparently told Charlie he wasn't going home, but he didn't say anything more. We have people searching the church and the surrounding area, and Kyle's mother is calling his friends."

"You thought he might come to me." He frowned, not sure he wanted to take hold of that idea.

"I was actually headed for the farm. Pastor Tim thought he might try to go there. And then I thought of you." Her face seemed so vulnerable as she looked up at him. "He admires you, you know."

He shook his head, not entirely sure what he was rejecting. "How would he get to the farm? Isn't it more likely he's hiding at the church?"

"If he is, they'll find him." She took a step away from him. "I'm going to check the farm. I'll let you know what happens."

Anger seemed to come from nowhere. "You think I'll just ignore the fact that a kid is missing? I'm coming with you." He beat her to the door. "Let's go."

In minutes, they were leaving Mt. Pleasant behind, headed north toward the farm. His fists clenched on his knees, feelings tumbling through him crazily.

"You think this is my fault, don't you?" The words shot out, carried by a gust of guilt and anger.

"No, of course I don't." Her gaze scanned the sides of the road as she drove.

He did the same, sweeping his eyes from side to side, as if he were searching gray waves for the sign of a survivor. "You wanted me to talk to Kyle. You think if I had that none of this would have happened."

"Stop telling me what I think." Annabel snapped the words right back at him. Then she shook her head, her lips trembling a little. "Please, Travis. There's no use in blaming ourselves. *If* you'd talked to him, *if* I'd talked to him, *if* Pastor Tim had gone to social services with your suspicion…none of that does any good now. We just have to find him. Then we'll sort the rest of it out."

She was probably right, but… "You don't think it's telling that Kyle ran away just when his father was due home?"

"I don't know. Maybe." She stared ahead, obviously straining to see the sides of the road in the near-dark.

He rubbed the back of his neck, unable to erase the tension. His throat was tight, but he knew he had to speak.

"It's not that I don't want to talk to the boy. I can't." His throat closed, and he shook his head. "I can't. That's the only way I know to deal with my past."

She didn't speak for a moment, flipping on the turn signal as the sign for the farm appeared ahead of them. "Miz Callie always says the past is for learning from, not for living in."

"I'm not. I don't." The thought sent a wave of revulsion through him. "That's the last thing I'd do."

He expected an argument. He didn't get it. Annabel slowed, turning into the lane.

"I would have said that, too." She drove slowly, leaning forward to watch the edges of the lane. "But as long as I let what happened two years ago affect what I do today, I am."

His jaw was so tight that it might have splintered. Did she really think her broken engagement compared to what he had endured? The moment he thought that, he seemed to hear it as if someone else had spoken. His heart had turned into a battleground.

Annabel's cell phone rang. She snatched it, stopping the car.

"Yes? All right. We'll come right away." She dropped the phone and jerked the wheel around to turn. "He's safe."

Travis closed his eyes for a second. "Thank God. Where?"

"He stowed away in Miz Callie's car." Annabel spun back out the lane toward the road. "She didn't discover him until she'd reached the beach house." She glanced at him. "Kyle begged her to call us before she got in touch with his parents. I said we'd come right away. Is that okay?"

Do you care enough to be involved in this? That was what she was really asking.

He wasn't sure of the answer. But he knew he couldn't run from the situation, not when a child's future was at stake.

"Yes."

Annabel's heart pounded in time with her footsteps as she hurried up the stairs to the beach house, with Travis right behind her. He had come, at least. Whether that would do any good, she didn't know.

Dear Lord, be with us now. Help us to understand what to do for this hurting child of Yours.

The door opened. Miz Callie stood framed in the opening, the light behind her making a halo of her white hair. She lifted a finger to her lips.

"He's in the kitchen," she said softly, "having some hot chocolate. Poor child was shaking. I don't know what's wrong, but I know a troubled child when I see one. Do you have any idea what's going on?"

Annabel clasped her grandmother's hands, feeling comfort and reassurance in Miz Callie's firm grip. "A little. Maybe now's the time he'll talk about it."

"I hope so." Miz Callie glanced from Annabel to Travis. "I called Pastor Tim when I heard your car. I couldn't delay any longer. I pray that's the right thing."

"Just keep on praying." She turned toward the kitchen and drew in a breath, her mind spinning. What could she say?

Travis caught her arm. "Wait. I'll do it." His face was a rigid mask, but a muscle twitched in his jaw, and pain moved in his eyes.

"You don't have to." Her heart hurt for him.

"Yes. I do." He walked away from her, into the kitchen, leaving the door open behind him as if to invite them to hear.

She watched Travis cross the familiar kitchen, pull out a chair and sit down next to Kyle. The boy gave him a quick, questioning glance and then stared down into his hot chocolate.

Annabel clasped her hands together, a wordless prayer forming in her heart. She felt Miz Callie's hands over hers and knew that her grandmother was praying, too.

"Seems like you had an adventure tonight, buddy." Travis's tone was casual, but Annabel could guess what that cost him.

Kyle hunched his shoulders.

"I guess you don't want to tell me why you ran away."

Kyle's body seemed to tense. Then he shook his head.

"Maybe I'll talk, then." Travis put one hand on the back of Kyle's chair, leaning close but not touching him. "You see, I think I know what's going on with you."

The hand on the chair tightened until the knuckles were white. Annabel held her breath.

"I was younger than you are when my dad started hitting me." By some effort of will, he kept his voice even. "At first it was because I did something wrong. So I tried to do everything just right, but that didn't seem like it did any good. Pretty soon it was every day, no matter what I did."

Kyle didn't move, but Annabel sensed he was listening with every fiber of his being. *Please,* her heart murmured. *Please.*

"You know, for a long time I figured it was my fault. I mean, if a guy's dad hits him all the time, there must be something wrong with the guy."

Pain stabbed at Annabel's heart. Why hadn't she seen that? Why hadn't she realized that a child would feel that way?

"It took a long time before I knew that it was my dad who had something wrong with him. But I kept quiet. I went on keeping quiet." Travis sucked in a breath, his chest heaving with the effort.

"I was wrong. All my life I've been wrong about that. I shouldn't have kept quiet about it then, because my dad needed help, and he didn't get it. And I shouldn't have been keeping quiet about it since then, because that hurt me." He touched his chest. "In here, it hurt me all the time, and I wouldn't admit it." He touched Kyle's chest, very lightly. "Does it hurt you in there, too?"

Kyle stared at him for a long moment. Then he nodded.

Annabel's tears spilled over onto her cheeks. *Thank You, Lord. Thank You.*

Travis brushed Kyle's hair back from his face very gently. "It's not right for your dad to hurt you. You know that, don't you?"

Kyle bit his lip. He turned his face away. And Annabel knew.

She moved forward and knelt by Kyle's chair, a wordless prayer filled her heart. "It's not your daddy who is hurting you, is it?"

Kyle shook his head, and tears rolled down his cheeks. "Not Daddy. Daddy never hurt me. It's Mamma."

Chapter Ten

On Christmas Eve, the Bodine family traditionally gathered at the beach house after the worship service. This year was no exception, but Annabel's feelings were mixed as she headed into the living room, which already seemed filled with siblings, cousins, aunts, uncles and in-laws.

The buzz of talk was nearly deafening, but maybe that was a good thing. She could smile, nod and think her own thoughts.

The past couple of days had gone in a blur of activity as she'd tried to help Pastor Tim with the ramifications of Kyle's words. Thank the good Lord all three of them had heard. Otherwise, Kyle might have recanted, either out of fear or some innate need to protect his mother.

With all that had been going on, there had seemed no opportunity for a private talk with Travis. Still, maybe that was how he'd wanted it.

She glanced toward where Travis stood at the far end of the room, a glass of eggnog in his hand, talking with Hugh. She'd have expected this gathering of the clan to overwhelm him, but he seemed perfectly at ease.

Miz Callie, standing at the laden buffet table, clinked a spoon against a glass, and everyone fell silent. In the glow of candles, her blue eyes shone as she looked at her family.

"Seems like we have a lot to be thankful for this Christmas. Let's pray."

Heads bowed around the room, and it was so quiet Annabel could hear the ticktock of the grandfather clock in the corner.

"Gracious Lord, we come before You on this Christmas Eve with our hearts filled with gratitude. This has been a year of change in our lives, and we're thankful for new beginnings and for new members. We welcome you to our family."

Annabel didn't need to look to know that Amanda was holding hands with Ross. Or that her cousin Adam had his arms around Cathy and Jamie, just as Georgia held tight to Matt and Lindsay.

"We're thankful to have my dear brother-in-law, Ned, returned to us after all these years." Miz Callie's voice was warm with thanksgiving that he was once more part of the family group. "And our hearts long for Luke and Cole, doing their duty far away. We pray your blessing on our dear friend Travis, joining us for the first time. Most of all, Lord, we thank You for the gift of Your dear Son, Whose birth we celebrate this night. In His name, Amen."

"Amen." The word echoed around the room.

Talk started up again, more muted now, like a comfortable hum filling in any lonely crevices in her heart.

People began to move toward the buffet table, with the usual exclamations about how lovely it was and who had brought what. She felt a hand on her arm and knew without looking that it was Travis. Her heart gave a little lurch, but she tried not to let any disturbance show in her face as she glanced up at him.

"Have a minute?" he asked. "I just wondered what the latest is on Kyle's situation."

"Pastor Tim and I were over at the house this afternoon. Don Morrison's mother arrived this morning, and she'll be staying indefinitely to take care of Kyle. I liked her right away—very warm and loving. Just what he needs, I'd say. And Don has managed to switch his job around so that he won't be traveling. I think he feels guilty that he didn't recognize just how wrong things were."

Travis's face tightened. "I'd have to agree with that. He should have."

"Sometimes people see only what they expect to see. And I think Kyle did an awfully good job of covering up for his mother."

"I guess so. What about her?"

"She's out of the house and going into therapy. I know it's not a perfect resolution, but at least it's a hopeful one."

Her own words gave her pause. Over the past two days, she'd begun to realize that her future might not include Travis. If so, she could still smile and go on. She could be content doing the work God had given her to do.

Travis nodded toward the buffet table. "If you're not set on eating right now, we could go outside and have a look at the stars, couldn't we?"

Her breath caught in her throat, and she nodded. "We could." She led the way to the sliding glass doors, and they stepped out onto the deck.

She crossed to the railing, looking out at the ocean, shimmering under a nearly full moon. The dark sky clustered with stars, so bright it seemed she should feel their heat on her face when she looked up. The breeze touched her skin, and the sand stretched out pale and empty below the deck. If she listened, she could hear the wind rustling in the sea oats in the dunes and the murmur of the waves on the shore, in and out in an endless progression.

God seemed very near, and she felt a flood of gratitude.

Travis stood next to her, his hands on the railing. He didn't speak. He just looked out at sea and sky.

But his hands clenched the rail until the veins stood out. He took a breath, audible in the stillness.

"You know, if there's anything I've learned through all this, it's the folly of keeping silent when something needs to be said."

It was almost an echo of what he'd told Kyle two nights ago. If he hadn't spoken then, they might all still be caught in a web of indecision over how to help the boy.

"Yes," she said when he didn't immediately go on. "I think you're right." She wanted to help him, but she didn't know how.

"For a long time I thought God had forgotten about me. It took coming here, being with all of you, to help me begin listening again. To find out that I was the one who'd moved away, not God."

"I'm glad," she said softly. If this knowledge was all she'd ever have of Travis, it was enough. "I've done a bit of learning myself. Realizing how foolish I was to close my heart because of someone who didn't care two pins about me. Realizing how fortunate I am to be in the place God wants me, doing the work He has for me."

"You told me something once that your grandmother said." He turned to face her, and her heart lurched. "That the past is for learning from, not for living in. I guess both of us had to find that out."

She nodded, her heart beating so fast that she didn't think she could trust herself to speak.

Travis took her hands in his, and his were warm and strong and protecting. His intent gaze probed her face. "We haven't known each other very long. Maybe you think it's too soon. But I don't have any doubt, Annabel. I know I love you."

Joy filled her, flooding through every separate cell of her body. This was what God had for her—the chance to love this man.

"I haven't known you long," she said. "But I know you through and through. And I know myself, as well. I love you, Travis McCall. I want to spend every Christmas of my life with you."

His arms went around her waist, and the love in his eyes took her breath away. "Every Christmas," he echoed. "Together." He bent, his warm breath crossing her lips. "Merry Christmas, Annabel. Merry Christmas."

* * * * *

Dear Reader,

After writing three books about the Bodine family of South Carolina, I am so delighted to have the opportunity to share a Christmas story about them with you. If you have read the other books, I hope you'll enjoy visiting with some of the characters again.

Annabel Bodine is the twin sister of Amanda, whose story I've already told. While I don't know what it's like to be a twin, I do know how close sisters can be, despite the fact that they can also be very different. I hope you'll enjoy getting better acquainted with Annabel, as she finds that love can meet her at Christmastime. Many of the details about Christmas events related to real activities in the Charleston area, and if you ever have the opportunity to visit Charleston at the holiday season, I hope you'll take it!

Please let me know how you felt about this story, and I'd love to send you a signed bookmark and my brochure of Pennsylvania Dutch recipes. You can write to me at Steeple Hill Books, 233 Broadway, Suite 1001, New York, NY 10279, e-mail me at marta@martaperry.com or visit me on the Web at www.martaperry.com.

Blessings,

Marta Perry

QUESTIONS FOR DISCUSSION

1. Can you understand why Travis was hesitant about sharing the Bodine family Christmas? Can you imagine how complicated his feelings about Christmas must be?

2. Annabel struggles with doubts about herself. Do you think her broken engagement is solely responsible for that? What else might contribute to her feelings?

3. Travis is so caught up in his anger over what happened to him in the past that he can't see his present clearly. How do you deal with it when you can't forget a hurt?

4. The Scripture verse for this story is one of my favorites. It never fails to strike awe in me when I say those words. What does it mean to you to know that you are a child of God?

5. Annabel tends to be shy in many situations, but she finds courage for the sake of the hurting children she helps. Have you ever found you're able to do things for others that you couldn't for yourself?

6. Miz Callie, the grandmother, is a voice for faith in all of the Bodine stories. Do you think you have someone in your life whom you can count on to be that?

7. With God's help, Annabel and Travis grow free of past hurts, able to love again. Are there any past hurts that hold you back in your life? What might you do about that?

THE GINGERBREAD SEASON

Betsy St. Amant

To my parents, for pointing me toward the true meaning of Christmas and making each holiday season special.

Acknowledgments

Special thanks to my husband, for not giving me too many weird looks for humming Christmas carols under my breath while I wrote this in early autumn, and to my sweet baby girl, for happily watching cartoons while Mommy worked on the laptop you still aren't allowed to touch.

As always, thanks to my agent, Tamela Hancock Murray, for being the world's greatest cheerleader and to my editor, Emily Rodmell, for your brainstorming and pushing to dig deeper.

Also, thanks to my grandmother Marie, for being an avid reader and patiently listening to all my various drafts of this story during those four-in-the-afternoon phone calls, and to Lori, for helping me throw candy canes— and eggs—as needed.

Then the angel said to them, "Do not be afraid, for behold, I bring you good tidings of great joy which will be to all people. For there is born to you this day in the city of David a Savior, who is Christ the Lord.

—*Luke* 2:10–11

Chapter One

The setting winter sun highlighted the familiar welcome sign in hues of pink and gold, ushering Allie James back into small-town life. The faded, carved stone greeting hadn't changed in the year since her last visit. *Welcome to Ginger Falls, Kansas—Population 7,504.* A grossly inaccurate count, as at least a fourth of those people had taken refuge in the neighboring big cities years ago, much like Allie had.

She brushed her curly dark hair from her face as she drove into the town's official limits—and straight into a blast from the past. The square was closed up for the night—what few shops were still open on Sunday, anyway—but Ginger Falls looked more like a ghost town than the thriving small community it'd once been. The red-and-white awning where she'd tossed her sister's favorite doll and gotten grounded for a week still hung over Jackson's Barbershop, but the white was more of a dirty yellow after years of wear. A laminated Closed sign hung on the door, and the windows were boarded up. Same with Bebe's Boutique.

And the gazebo. Allie slowed down as she passed the once glorious structure in the center of Ginger Falls. The pristine white columns were stained and worn, the bench where many sat telling secrets or pledging love, crippled and broken. Ignored, forgotten.

She leaned on the accelerator and sped past the bad memories.

Some were better off ignored, forgotten.

A few minutes later, Allie left Ginger Falls in her wake and hit the country highway leading to her parents' house. The dark road snaked through a wide expanse of wheat fields, a shadowy intruder against the sea of plants tinted silver with frost. Allie's childhood home, smack in the middle of the state's largest Christmas-tree farm, beckoned even from miles away, a safe harbor in the midst of the chaos churning in her mind. She wasn't the first twenty-eight-year-old to lose her job and move back home—but that didn't ease the rock of regret in her stomach. If she'd listened to her parents' advice and accepted that position at the consulting firm in Kansas City instead of working at an independent bookstore, she might still have a job—and an apartment.

Now she had neither.

Allie exited the highway and turned down the long

gravel road. Her two-door car bumped along and rattled her teeth. She wished for the shock-absorbing truck she used to drive as a teenager. She steered around a pothole and winced. Those memories weren't any better, because like the gazebo, most of her thoughts about her old truck also centered on Jordan Walker. Carpooling to school their senior year, driving through the trails of the Christmas-tree farm on her parents' property, sitting on the tailgate under the stars. Everyone told Allie growing up that her senior year would fly by, but she hadn't realized how true that was until she looked up one day after graduation and realized she'd fallen for Jordan even faster.

The porch lamp of her parents' two-story cottage shone through the twilight and illuminated the shadows as Allie pulled her car up the winding drive. She parked behind her father's work truck and drew a deep breath. Home again. Though this time, it wasn't because of the coming Christmas holiday. This time, it was with her tail between her legs, needing food and shelter because she was a failure. It might not directly be her fault the bookstore went under, but surely she could have done more, worked harder— *something* to keep her job afloat. She'd devoted several years to learning the inner workings of the business, in the hope of starting her own store one day. Now it seemed it was for nothing.

Nerves pinched Allie's stomach as she slid out

of her car and shouldered her duffel bag and purse. What would her parents think of her? Her dad had every right to say "I told you so," and her mother would probably give her that straight-lipped look that testified to all the admonitions she struggled to restrain. They'd probably be counting the dollars she could have earned by now if she'd taken the sure road instead of the risky one.

Allie shivered in the cold evening air. Might as well get it over with so they could figure out a way to make this work. She loved her parents, but she wasn't naive enough to think that coming home would be easy on any of them. She'd almost given up hope of the business loan she'd applied for being approved back in Kansas City. It wasn't the best time for banks to take risks, and despite her hardworking intentions of opening her own store, that's exactly what she was. Until she could build up her savings, she had nowhere else to go but home—even if home was the very place that held all of her worst memories.

With knuckles white against the strap of her duffel, Allie made her way over the snow-dusted stepping stones toward the porch, the weight of her failures resting on her tired shoulders.

So much for having the best Christmas ever.

Allie dropped a handful of marshmallows into the mug of hot chocolate and watched them melt. She stirred it with a candy cane, her mother's favorite holiday signature, and tried to smile.

"We missed you last Christmas." Her father's thick brows furrowed as he leaned back in his chair across the table. Dave James had always been a broad bear of a man, thankfully more teddy than grizzly. He shook his head. "It wasn't the same, even with your sister, Molly, and her family here."

"I know, and I'm sorry. I hated to miss it, but I was busy with the bookstore." The words caught in Allie's throat, and she quickly took a sip to wash them down. The store that no longer existed—partially because of her. She waited for her dad's disapproving comment, but he remained surprisingly silent.

Her mother, Karen, patted Allie's arm. "This year will make up for all that. Maybe you won't have to go back after all."

Allie shook her head. "Mom, you know I'm only here long enough to get back on my feet. I have a life in Kansas City." One she desperately wanted to return to. She'd escaped this town once before because of Jordan Walker and her crumbling relationship with her parents, and she wasn't about to get sucked back into the past. At least Jordan wouldn't be here to make this Christmas even more awkward. Last she'd heard, Jordan had started an Internet business and was enjoying his success on the West Coast.

Apparently all the dreams he'd imagined for himself had come true.

While hers wasted away like the last leaves of autumn.

Her mother fluttered one hand in the air. "There's no hurry. I'd love for you to stay. It'd give me another woman to talk to out here in the middle of the nowhere, what with Molly staying so busy with her catering business."

Exhaling slowly, Allie counted to ten. Everything always went back to Molly—the firstborn, the favorite. The rivalry between Allie and her sister had only grown worse as they got older, mostly due to their mother's constant, tactless comments. Of the few things Allie missed about her hometown, that definitely wasn't one of them. "I appreciate the offer to hang around, Mom, but I'll be heading back to Kansas City as soon as I can." *It won't be soon enough.*

"Your mother's right. Don't rush on our account." Dad leaned back in his chair, the buttons of his flannel shirt straining over his burgeoning stomach. "I do, however, appreciate your being self-sufficient."

"*Used* to be self-sufficient." Allie muttered into her mug. She reached for the newspaper lying on the table in an effort to change the subject and flipped to the thin Classifieds. "Have you heard of any jobs available around town?"

Her father exhaled. "It's a tough economy right now. You know that."

Yes, Allie knew that—the economy was largely what caused the bookstore to close. Business slowed until the owner, Tammy, couldn't afford to keep both Allie and the weekend help. Everything spiraled downward from there, and the attempts Allie made at advertising and marketing completely flopped— as Tammy not-so-kindly informed her the day she announced the shop was closing.

Dad took a long drink from his mug. "That's why we're not expecting you to blaze out of here as quickly as you think you might. These things take time."

Time she couldn't afford to waste. The sooner Allie landed some paychecks, the sooner she could get back to Kansas City—and more importantly, away from the reminders of her past. The gazebo flashed through her mind, and she inwardly winced.

"What's this?" Allie pointed to an ad in the bottom corner of the paper. "Community Renewal Program Director Needs Immediate Assistant. Full-time, Temporary. Contact 555-JOBS for information."

"Oh, that's right." Mom leaned forward and tapped the paper with a manicured nail. "Ginger Falls has a Community Renewal Program now. Mayor Cubley and the city council just hired a director. Apparently this man has several plans in place to revive the town. It's just what we've been needing."

Allie raised her eyebrows in surprise. From her drive through Main Street earlier, it seemed like the town needed more of a miracle than a remodel. But a job was a job. "I've got secretarial experience. Maybe I'll give the job agency a call." Hope bloomed in Allie's heart like a holiday poinsettia. Maybe this Christmas wouldn't turn out quite so dismal after all.

Jordan Walker shuffled through the paperwork on his desk, looking for the list of appointments he'd scheduled for the day. He was glad the new assistant the job agency hired for him would be arriving any minute, but he was more than a little embarrassed he'd misplaced the piece of paper with the woman's name on it. She was starting not a minute too soon— his progress already threatened to be lost in a sea of disorganization. Two weeks ago, he'd rented office space on Main Street, which served as his first step in renewing Ginger Falls. The two-story complex sat abandoned these past several years after a group of lawyers moved on, and the loft was perfect space for his office. The narrow windows on the north wall offered a view of Main Street, which, on bad days, would hopefully remind him of his goal—to restore Ginger Falls to its original glory, back to the way the town had been when he'd grown up—to the days of fellowship and camaraderie, where everyone knew everyone and children were safe to roam the streets and eat ice cream cones. The community desperately needed a makeover, and he was just the person to do it. His time in California had shown him the things that mattered most, and his hometown was now at the top of his priority list.

Hopefully the agency had been picky. If the two interviews he conducted himself before turning the job over to them was any indication, he'd have never gotten a decent secretary. One prospect had been fresh out of high school, and her first question was if tattoos and piercings were okay. Then during a phone interview with another prospect, he'd had to repeat himself six times because of a broken hearing aid. Neither applicant seemed to mesh with his vision for Ginger Falls. He needed someone efficient and energetic, someone who could be his partner and share the same goal for the town. Someone who believed in his dream.

"Jordan?"

His stomach flipped, and he looked at the door. But the curly haired, slim-figured image in the door frame didn't vanish. The automatic greeting he formed stuck in his throat, and he quickly rose to his feet, legs trembling with shock. "Allie James?" He cleared his throat, drinking in the sight of his most bittersweet memory.

Her eyes, as blue as he'd always remembered, were

wide as she braced one hand against the wall, as if holding herself upright. Jordan felt a little off balance himself. He squared his shoulders, trying to regain even an ounce of the professionalism that usually came so naturally. "Nice to see you." The words sounded dry, even to his own ears. But what was he supposed to say to the woman he once thought he'd marry?

Her dark curls brushed against her shoulders as she rapidly shook her head in disbelief. "You're the director of the Community Renewal Program?"

"That's what's on my nameplate," Jordan joked, trying to lighten the tension that stretched between them. He gestured to the chair across from his desk. "I take it you're my new assistant. Have a seat." He fought the urge to rake his hand through his dark hair, a nervous habit he refused to show.

Allie hesitated, then nodded. "Thank you." She settled into the chair and smoothed her skirt over her legs. But her shocked expression betrayed her prim posture.

He could relate. His own smile felt plastered with surprise. Jordan eased back into his own seat, trying not to stare. Time had done little to change Allie's beauty. In fact, it might have even enhanced it. He steepled his fingers on his desk. "So, Allie…" Her name felt foreign on his lips, and he cleared his throat. "How've you been?"

"Good." She fiddled with a piece of lint from her skirt.

Jordan sat back in his chair and tried to look casual, hoping Allie would follow his lead and relax. Her back was held so straight and rigid that she had to be getting a cramp by now. "It's been…years."

"Ten, to be exact." She looked up, her eyes holding a pointed challenge.

Jordan nearly smiled at the hint of her old spark. No matter the subtle barb was pointed straight at him. He neatly dodged it. "Right. So, where'd you end up after graduation? The community college?" He might be hitting too close to their infamous moment in history, but if she was going to be his new secretary, he needed to know her background.

Or at least that was his excuse.

Allie drew a deep breath. "Actually, I went to the University of Kansas and majored in business."

She'd left town for school. The realization slapped Jordan across the face. The argument that precipitated their breakup that fateful night had been based on how they wanted different things—he'd wanted to go to university, as his parents wanted, and Allie had wanted to go to the local community college and then work for her family's Christmas-tree farm. They'd been two different people on two very different paths. Jordan quickly brushed aside the negativity toward his family. Everything had worked out for the best.

"I spent the last three years working for an independent bookstore in Kansas City that recently went under." Allie leaned forward in her chair. "I have plans of opening my own bookstore and coffee shop soon. So it seemed a temporary job here was ideal." She hesitated. "It *is* temporary, right?"

"Yes, it is. I just need someone through the holidays." Jordan nodded slowly in an attempt to hide his surprise. Who would have guessed small-town Allie James would have been living life in a big city all these years? Last he'd heard, she'd planned on staying in Ginger Falls forever—only one of the obstacles in their past relationship, though perhaps the biggest. What would have happened if, at eighteen years old, he'd chosen Allie over his planned future? What irony. He'd gone away to fulfill his parents' dreams and left his own at the town gazebo that chilly Christmas Eve night.

Allie stared at him, and Jordan realized with a start he'd been quiet much longer than he'd realized. He quickly tried to recollect his train of thought. "It sounds like you'll be a great asset to my vision for Ginger Falls. The agency made a good choice." Jordan waited a beat and then lowered his voice. "But, Allie, if this is too weird, I understand. I don't want things to be awkward between us."

He held his breath, waiting for a sign, anything to indicate her interest. Somehow, he needed her to take this position, and that need stemmed from something more than a desperate requirement of a competent secretary.

But for now he refused to acknowledge what it was.

Chapter Two

He'd grown at least two inches since senior year.
Allie clenched her purse in her lap and tried not to
stare at the dusky shadow covering Jordan's chiseled jaw and the way his dark hair waved to perfection over his forehead as he waited for her response.
Attractive or not, this was Jordan Walker—the man
who broke her heart as a freshman in college and
ruined Christmas for her.

But she desperately needed this job. And the
agency probably wouldn't be nearly as understanding as Jordan seemed to be if she refused the position. It was a guaranteed paycheck—if she could just
focus on the present and ignore the painful memories
of the past. She finally nodded. "It's fine, Jordan.
Things won't be too weird at all."

Unable to mask the relieved sigh that floated from
his lips, Jordan said, "Great. You won't regret this,
Allie." His gaze met and held with hers, and she

drew a shaky breath before looking away, out the window.

"I'm not sure how much the agency told you, but I need someone in the office and out in the field with me five days a week, regular hours. You'd be doing secretarial work—filing, organizing, things like that—when we're not planning various events."

Her eyes darted back to his. "Out in the field?"

"Out there." He pointed to the window. "Your job will be helping me coordinate and carry out events that will bring revenue back into Ginger Falls— starting with the Gingerbread Festival the week of Christmas."

"I thought they hadn't done that festival in years." Not since she'd graduated from college. Memories of brightly lit store windows danced before her eyes like sugarplums. The festival used to be the talk of the town, the one event everyone looked forward to all year.

"All the more reason to bring it back. Restoring Ginger Falls has become my mission." Jordan stood and walked to the window, one hand resting against the glass pane as he stared out at Main Street. "Weeks ago, I proposed this restoration plan to the city council. The mayor and council approved a small stipend to help me get things going, but I'm also donating some of my own money. I see it as a temporary investment for a good cause."

"This town definitely needs some help." She

couldn't argue with that. "But what if you invest money into trying to get Ginger Falls back on the map and you fail?"

"Then I move on and try something else." Jordan shrugged as he turned to face her. "That's what business is about—risk. I wouldn't have been successful with my architectural design company if I hadn't gone out on a limb now and then." He grinned, and Allie's heart thudded like she was seventeen all over again. "And trust me, a few of those limbs were quite wobbly."

"I see." But she didn't, not really. It was a worthy cause to restore Ginger Falls, but why did Jordan care so much?

The phone on the desk rang, and Jordan held up one finger. "I'm sorry. Excuse me just a moment." He answered, then he spoke in hushed tones.

Allie watched the broad lines of his back as he angled toward the wall. It was so strange to see the boy she'd once loved now a man—her boss, at that. Could she really work for someone who once shattered her heart? Someone who'd almost ruined her favorite holiday?

Jordan's cell buzzed on his hip, and still on the landline, he reached to check the caller ID. His elbow knocked a pile of papers off his desk in the process, and they fluttered onto the floor.

Instinctively, Allie jumped up and started gathering the papers. Jordan's lack of organization apparently hadn't changed. He really did seem to need help. Her resolve strengthened. Somehow, seeing his vulnerable side made things a little easier. She returned the papers to Jordan's desk as he hung up the phone.

"Thanks. Sorry about that." He exhaled. "It's been crazy lately, but that's good, right? It means things are happening." Jordan smiled, and her stomach flipped like a pancake. He held out his hand. "Welcome aboard, Allie."

She stared at Jordan's outstretched hand beneath the long sleeve of his charcoal suit coat. The color darkened his eyes, and they seemed to flicker with something much more dangerous than her current state of unemployment.

She brushed the hair out of her eyes, stalling for time. What had Jordan said about risk? She forced her hand in his and shook it firmly before she could change her mind. "Thanks, Boss."

Jordan struggled to identify the feelings in his gut as Allie hurried out of his office. There was relief that he had a new assistant, regret over the way things had ended with him and Allie so many years ago and a nervous flutter that made him think things weren't quite as over as he'd thought. Time had seemed to stand still when she walked in the room, parading a line of memories through his mind as if they were both back in high school, cheering from the stands at the football game. Sharing French fries at the local diner. Arguing over which movie to rent on Saturday night.

He sighed as he made another attempt to straighten the chaos on his desk. At least she'd agreed to take the job. Maybe that was a good sign that they could try to be friends again. They agreed to start fresh the next morning, allowing Allie time to settle in at her parents' house before diving into work.

It wasn't easy getting started in the world. Jordan knew he'd been fortunate—no, blessed—to have come as far as he had. He'd gone from a college graduate with nothing more than dreams and a laptop to a successful businessman with a large warehouse in California, stores all over the West Coast and an Internet business that practically ran itself. Who knew his architectural degree would have led him into the world of home design? A degree he now hoped would help him bring Ginger Falls— financially and physically—back to life.

Though he'd never have guessed it would have cost him his first love.

Jordan slumped in his desk chair and buried his face in his hands. Somewhere along the way, his family's dreams had become his own, yet none of them—his parents, or grandparents—were around to see his success. His grandparents had passed away years ago, and his parents had divorced and relocated to other states. Somehow, Jordan had to leave a legacy in Ginger Falls—to make his past worth the effort.

To make it worth losing Allie.

The gazebo drew Allie like a kid to a cookie jar— even though she knew the punishment to come. She parked at an empty meter and slid out of her car. The white structure rose above her in the center of town square, a notorious reminder of crushed dreams.

She stood on the first step, noted the broken board on the second and ran one gloved hand over the stained, chipped column. In her mind's eye, however, the gazebo remained pristine and fresh, the way it had looked ten years ago when she'd eagerly come to meet Jordan. It was the first time they'd be together in person since parting ways for college, and Allie knew it would be the moment Jordan finally professed his love. They'd dated exclusively but never spoken the big *L*-word. She'd hoped it'd be his Christmas gift to her. After he left town for college, she'd been concerned about their relationship. Jordan had grown distant, and she'd prayed it was just because of his busy new schedule. She couldn't ever quite decipher his sudden lack of attention.

But he'd made it all too clear Christmas Eve night.

Allie's gaze drifted to the broken bench. She'd thought she and Jordan would snuggle together that cold evening and whisper promises of love. She'd arrived early, taking the bus so she could ride with Jordan to get dinner later, and waited with all the anticipation the holiday could offer. But Jordan had showed up moody, having argued with his parents, and told Allie he couldn't handle the pressure anymore. He was tired of his family hounding him, tired of being unable to keep everyone in his life happy. Something had to give.

And that something had been Allie.

He'd offered to take her home, but she'd ran off, tears blinding her eyes, preferring to freeze than ride in his truck one last time. She'd called her father, and her dad had taken one look at Allie's chattering teeth and icy tears and turned the heater on full blast. Then he'd said, "You can let a boy ruin your favorite holiday, or you can be in charge of making your own happy memories."

Those were the only words he'd spoken the entire drive home, and she'd never forgotten them since. With her favorite holiday CD blasting from her stereo, she'd thrown out every memento of her and Jordan and declared herself officially over him. Yet every time she heard "Jingle Bells" or saw a brightly lit tree stuffed full of shiny ornaments, memories of his rejection threatened to overwhelm her Christmas spirit.

"Ten years ago," Allie whispered as she stared at the gazebo, halfway wishing her anger would melt the snow covering the crumbling bench. But it didn't matter. It was ancient history. Now she was Jordan's employee, but if she didn't guard her heart, history would very likely repeat itself.

She turned and walked to her car. She'd learned from her mistakes and realized putting all her hopes in Jordan Walker was without a doubt the biggest mistake of her life. She might have to work with him for a few weeks, but she didn't have to love him again—or even like him, for that matter. She'd do this job for the money, as she would for any other employer, then hightail it back to Kansas City as fast as she could.

Leaving history safely tucked away in the past.

Chapter Three

The stacks from yesterday had doubled. Allie winced as she cast a glance over the piles of papers and folders on Jordan's desk. Where had it all come from? She dropped her jacket and purse on the chair—the only clean surface available—and hesitated. "Jordan?"

Or should she call him Mr. Walker? He was, after all, her new boss. Allie wrinkled her nose. Professionalism or not, it would be impossible to address by last name the man she'd once kissed. "Jordan, are you here?"

The closet door, partially open, cracked farther, and Jordan stepped into the room. His dark suit jacket hung open over a stiff dress shirt and black slacks. Allie looked down at her jeans and pullover green sweater. She'd forgotten to ask about a dress code and instead, had dressed to work, to move boxes and files.

He shut the closet door. "Hey, there. I was just starting to file."

"You mean there was more than this a few minutes ago?" She gestured toward the desk with amazement.

Jordan grinned. "Actually, I meant I was starting the process of locating the filing cabinet."

Allie pointedly checked her watch. "You do realize our workday is only eight hours?" Her stomach quivered at the thought of working beside Jordan all day long—for the next several weeks. She tried to cling to her earlier resolve.

"Yes. And now you realize why I'm paying so much." There was that infamous smile again, dimpling his left cheek and turning down slightly on the right side.

Allie quickly averted her stare. *Stay away from the dimples.* She drew a deep breath and pretended to search through her purse for a pen. *God, my memories of Jordan and how things ended between us was hard enough. Being in the same room together now is too much. Could You drop a few thousand dollars from the sky this time to pay my bills instead?*

She glanced over her shoulder, and Jordan held up a pen. "Looking for one of these?"

Or better yet, could You just take those dimples away altogether?

Allie accepted the pen and steeled herself. "Thanks." Maybe helping Jordan meet his goals for

Ginger Falls would alleviate the gnawing ache in her stomach that reminded her of her own failures—and distract from the high school girl inside of her that wanted to jump back into Jordan's arms as if nothing had ever changed.

She settled into the chair by the desk and reached for the first towering stack, determined to stay busy and keep thoughts of kissing—and dimples—at bay. "What is all this, anyway?"

"I created profiles on all the local businesses and the available properties for sale or rent." Jordan pointed to the scanner/fax machine in the corner of the office. "The merchants filled out the profiles for me, but I need to get them into the computer."

Allie flipped through the pages. "Great. I'll just finish organizing this system you've got going so far and get started typing."

Jordan hesitated, and Allie couldn't help but giggle. "You don't *have* a system, do you?"

"I told you, I just realized the filing cabinet was in the closet." He sheepishly rubbed the back of his neck with one hand. "I haven't been set up in here for very long."

Allie uncapped the pen, fighting the smile that hovered beneath the surface of her lips. Some things never changed. "Then you might want to consider ordering in lunch."

Jordan tossed his empty sandwich container into the trash. He'd managed to wolf the ham and cheese down in between various phone calls, but Allie's half-eaten lunch still sat beside her on the desk—which she had completely cleared in the four hours since she'd started work. Every few minutes, she'd reach over and absently take a bite of pickle from her plate and rub her fingers over her jeans then go back to the list she was making.

He suddenly felt useless in his own office. No doubt if Allie got the loan she sought in Kansas City, she'd be able to create a successful business of her own. She'd already worked wonders here.

Yet dismay tainted Jordan's joy of being able to once again see his desk. If Allie was this efficient, she'd be out of a job by the time Christmas rolled around, which was probably exactly what she wanted. She'd made it clear during the interview that this job was temporary for her as well, and she had every intention of moving back to Kansas City. What happened to make her so eager to leave the city she once swore she never would? He'd be arrogant to assume their breakup had given her that kind of motivation. Something else had to have happened. He swallowed the lump in his throat. He realized breaking up with her had cost him not only love but his best friend.

He watched as Allie took a long drink from her soda. That night at the gazebo had been the worst fight they'd ever had. He hadn't intended to actually break up, but Allie's lack of understanding about his family's pressure on him had pushed him over the edge. She'd left the gazebo first, practically shoving him down the stairs in her rush to get away. He'd hurried to follow her, but she'd blazed a trail through the snow toward the highway. No way was he letting her walk miles to her house—but when her father's car pulled over on the side of the street, Jordan knew he'd lost any chance of convincing her he still loved her.

Sort of like any chance of them being able to rekindle their friendship now. Allie had spoken a total of three sentences to him the first two hours they worked together. When he offered her coffee, she had said thanks and gone silent. Then she'd asked where the restroom was, and later on, she requested that he turn up the thermostat.

Jordan studied the way her curly dark hair grazed her cheek as she furiously scribbled on her project. She'd changed since high school—for the better. She seemed stronger now, not the clingy girlfriend she'd once been. Her smile, however, hadn't changed a bit—it could still brighten a midnight sky and send bolts of lightning through his body.

Too bad she wasn't smiling at him more often. He'd recognized that familiar spark of hers once today, earlier in the morning when she finished the filing and shut the closet door with a satisfied gleam of accomplishment in her eye. But the moment her gaze had landed on his, she'd stiffened and busied herself with the next task on her list. Despite her earlier claims of their partnership not being weird, it obviously was.

Regardless of what was going on in Allie's head, and the awkwardness between them, Jordan couldn't keep sitting here staring at her—even if the view was the best he'd seen in a long time. "Need anything?"

She shook her head, not even bothering to glance up.

He tried again. "You've barely touched your lunch."

She shrugged. "Wouldn't kill me to lose a few pounds."

"I think you look great."

Allie looked up, one eyebrow arched.

Jordan mentally kicked himself. It was hardly professional to be doling out compliments, even if they were true. He frantically backpedaled. "You know what I mean. No signs of that infamous 'freshman fifteen' from college life." He mentally kicked himself. *Good one, man.*

Allie's lips pressed together. "It was actually twenty pounds, but thanks for bringing that up."

Heat burned his cheeks. "I'm sorry, I just—"

"I'm kidding."

He breathed a sigh so heavy his breath fanned the pages of Allie's list. Then he slumped in his chair.

Allie's eyes narrowed. "So you actually believed I

gained twenty pounds since high school? Do I look that much bigger to you?"

Panic seized Jordan's senses. "No, not at all, I—"

A smile broke through the storm clouds on Allie's face and she laughed. "Got you again."

Jordan clutched his heart through his shirt. "Funny." About as funny as a heart attack, but he forced a smile for Allie's sake.

"Now let me finish what I'm doing before I lose my train of thought." She bent back over her paperwork.

"Yes, ma'am." He walked over to the window, breathing a relieved sigh as he gazed over Main Street. If Allie was teasing him and making jokes, then perhaps she felt more comfortable in his presence. Maybe, given time, there'd even be hope of friendship again.

He glanced over his shoulder at Allie, still hard at work, and whispered a prayer toward the heavens. *Lord, if You're still in the miracle business, then Ginger Falls could really use one. And so could I.*

Allie clenched her pen as she tried to concentrate on her list, but her stomach growled in protest. She quickly finished the last of her chips and then threw the empty bags away before sitting down. She forced a smile, despite Jordan's turned back at the window. "The filing is done, your desk is clean and I've made a list of advertising ideas for the upcoming fundraisers." Hopefully those ideas would work better than the plans she'd created for the bookstore that closed. She quickly opened the laptop on Jordan's desk. Even though she'd probably not gotten her loan, eventually she'd show everyone what she could do.

Jordan turned from the window. "Great. Let's see what you have."

"Do you want to look them over while I type these notes into a spreadsheet?" She handed Jordan the blue folder full of papers. "That way everything will be done today, and we can start work on the Gingerbread Festival tomorrow."

Jordan took the folder from her outstretched hand. "Sounds good. The festival is definitely the most pertinent. If it doesn't raise some money and glean interest from the surrounding communities, then we'll have to change tactics for any events we host next year."

"I'll do my best to help make it a success." The last thing she needed was any more failures on her record.

"Of course. I have every faith you will." Jordan smiled and began to flip through the notes, his brow furrowing as he read. "You've got some good stuff here. A few of these ideas I'd thought of as well, like going door-to-door in the community and telling shop owners in person what we need from them. But ordering pens and buttons with the Gingerbread Festival dates printed on them is a great idea, and so is asking the local merchants to contribute giveaways for door prizes at the festival."

Allie wished his compliments didn't matter so much. But her heart soaked them in like cool rain on a hot, dusty field. "Great. I'll try to come up with more."

"This gives us a good head start. In the meantime, we need to start discussing ideas for a finale for the end of the festival." Jordan tapped the notebook with his finger before tossing it on the desk. "Something really catchy and newsworthy, to get extra publicity for Ginger Falls."

"Sounds good." Allie jotted a note down on a piece of paper. "I'll start thinking about that."

"Why don't we go brainstorm together over some ice cream—my treat."

Surely he didn't mean this as a date? "Ice cream? It's practically snowing outside."

Jordan plucked his coat off the hook behind the door and shrugged his arms into it. "Random dessert trips are a perk of the job. Did the agency forget to mention that when they hired you?" He grinned. "Come on. Grab your jacket. Maybe something genius will strike us after we've had sprinkles and brain freeze."

"Okay, if you're sure." Allie slid into her coat and followed Jordan out the door into the cold.

But her heart felt a little warmer already.

Chapter Four

"Dad, you didn't have to wait for me." Allie followed her father's boot prints in the snow as they trudged through the maze of Christmas trees on her parents' property. The December air nipped at her cheeks. "I know you and Mom usually put your tree up right after Thanksgiving."

"Your mother insisted, and I agreed. We missed you last Christmas. This one needs to be extra special. The more traditions we can share, the better." Her father adjusted the ax on his shoulder and peered back to study a tall spruce. "What do you think?"

"It's a beauty. But all your trees are first-class."

"Is it green enough?" He frowned.

"It's perfect." Like her ice cream trip with Jordan earlier that afternoon. She kicked the crusty snow at her feet while her dad began to chop at the tree's trunk. It'd be easier on her heart if Jordan was an arrogant snob who couldn't care less about her anymore—like the man she'd pictured he'd become after all this time. But he'd looked into her eyes over a sprinkled cone of vanilla crunch and really seemed interested in what she'd been doing in the years they'd been apart. And, rather reluctantly, she found herself caring about him in the same way.

"How was your first day on the job?" Her father grunted as he swung the ax a third time. Sweat broke out on his brow line below his knit hat.

"Productive." Allie stepped aside as the tree began to lean toward the path. "I'll be busy these next few weeks, especially with the Gingerbread Festival coming up. I think it's going to be really fun this year."

"Good. I always liked that event." The ax swung faster. "Your mom told me Jordan is your new boss."

Allie stared at her gloved hands. "It is a little awkward." That was an understatement—like saying snow was a little cold.

"I'm sure if your mother had realized who the director was, she would have warned you the other night." Dad straightened before giving the trunk a final blow. The tree crashed to the ground, its branches wobbling and scattering tidbits of ice on impact. "But it seems like it's turning out okay."

She briefly closed her eyes before forcing a smile. "Right." If "okay" meant emotional exhaustion from trying to remind herself she and Jordan were long over, then sure, things had turned out "okay." "It's just that…" Allie broke off, rolling in her lower lip.

"What?"

"Nothing." She'd never been comfortable talking to her father about boys as a teenager, and somehow this didn't seem the best time to start.

He shoved his hat back on his head and squinted. "You're not going to let this ruin your Christmas again, are you?"

"No, Dad." Allie sighed. "I didn't the first time, and I won't this time either."

"Good. I'm glad to hear my advice doesn't go stale over the years." Her father huffed as he dragged the tree onto the sled he'd built for that very purpose. He handed Allie one of the two long leather straps and grinned. "Now pull."

Wednesday morning, Allie parked her car on Main Street and sighed. As much as she enjoyed their impromptu ice cream run yesterday, Allie hoped Jordan planned to keep things more professional today. Somehow, she had to keep the emotions he provoked deep inside and find a way to be his business partner—and maybe eventually a friend again.

If only her memories would cooperate.

Allie's door opened before she could even reach

for the handle, and Jordan smiled down at her from the street. "Good morning."

"Hi." She allowed his assistance from the car, wincing as she stepped on his loafer with her boot. "Sorry."

Jordan handed her a red thermos full of coffee. "Just the way you like it. Or the way you liked it yesterday at the office, at least."

"Thanks. This is unexpected." She took the thermos and inhaled the steam escaping from the lid. Maybe the caffeine would give her strength to get through the day and keep her goals close at hand.

"You're very welcome." Jordan gestured toward the town as Allie took a long sip. "I thought today we'd go door-to-door on Main Street and make sure the existing shop owners know about the upcoming Gingerbread Festival and are willing to participate. We also need to spread the word about the big finale you came up with yesterday." Jordan smiled. "That was a really good idea. I can't wait to see the picture."

"A picture taken from a plane of the townspeople standing in the shape of a gingerbread man?" Allie laughed nervously. "I think maybe I had too much sugar yesterday. Are we sure that's going to work?"

"Of course. I've already made some calls to some local pilots for prices. I think it'll be a great draw for families. What kid wouldn't want a chance to be part of the state's largest gingerbread man and get a free picture?"

True. She'd have loved to do that as a child.

"So don't doubt yourself. It was a great idea."

"Thanks." She smiled, her shoulders loosening as she drank in the gratitude in his eyes. Then she caught herself and looked away. Jordan's opinion of her shouldn't matter so much. But she couldn't stop the warm glow in her stomach.

"Shall we?" Jordan gestured toward Theo's Diner across the street.

"Sure." Allie shivered as a gust of wind tickled her hair. "Just let me grab my scarf. I'd forgotten how much colder it is here than in Kansas City." She set the thermos of coffee on the roof of her car, then took her favorite blue-and-green scarf from her purse and wrapped it around her neck.

Jordan laughed. "Trust me, after spending some time on the West Coast for my business, it was definitely culture shock coming back."

"I can imagine." Allie studied Jordan from the corner of her eye as she retrieved her thermos and fell into step beside him. She always knew Jordan would be destined for great things. Despite his family's support, he had always doubted himself in high school, and their senior year, he almost didn't even fill out applications for college. Did he remember she was the one who talked him into going for his dreams?

A lot of good that did her. Jordan had gotten success, the town had gotten a potential legend and she'd gotten a broken heart.

"Here we are." Jordan reached behind Allie to open the door of Theo's Diner, the tinkling bell jarring her from her dismal thoughts. She quickly stepped over the threshold, determined not to let memories overcome her this early in the day.

"Theo, are you here?" Jordan called over the counter. Allie's stomach grumbled as the aroma of eggs, bacon and buttered toast floated from the kitchen. The diner had a total of three customers for breakfast. What a shame. If the hearty smells were any indication, Theo was still as good a cook as he'd been the last time Allie stopped by over a year ago.

"Jordan! You want the usual, kid?" Theo's balding head popped through the opening. The top half of his apron was already covered in grease.

"Not today, Theo. We can't stay. Maybe some powdered doughnuts to go? I just need to talk to you for a minute." Jordan placed his hand on Allie's shoulder. "You remember Allie?"

Theo beamed as he made his way around the partition and through the swinging door to the counter. "The James girl! Who could forget?" He slapped the counter with both hands. "You want doughnuts, too?"

Allie opened her mouth to answer, but the weight

of Jordan's hand on her arm robbed her of speech. She nodded, her cheeks burning almost as hot as her shoulder.

Theo shot Jordan a confused look before reaching for a paper bag and the pastry tongs.

"Allie is my new employee. We're heading up the Ginger Falls Community Renewal Program, starting with the annual Gingerbread Festival. You game this year?"

"I always loved that festival." Theo folded the top of the white sack and stapled it. "Count me in. What do you need?"

Jordan casually moved his arm away from Allie, and she breathed for the first time since the conversation started. "Just your sponsorship and support. Local establishments will get free publicity in exchange for donating to the event. Any snacks you could provide during the week would be appreciated, and if it's all right, we'll need to post some flyers in here for advertising."

Theo's chest puffed as he handed over the bag. "Not a problem. I'm happy to do my part." Jordan reached for his wallet, and Theo waved him off. "On the house. Think of it as my first act of sponsorship."

"Thank you." Allie chimed in, wanting to participate in the conversation at least once before they left. "That means a lot."

Theo's cheeks tinged red. "Anything for my

town—even if it's only feeding two of its nicest people."

"Thanks again." Jordan gave Allie the doughnuts and swiped several napkins from the container on the counter. "We'll be in touch with the details and the flyers."

Theo waved as he headed back into the kitchen. Allie hurried toward the door to open it first and avoid another ungraceful moment of ducking under Jordan's arm. Her shoulder still burned from his contact. She hated that after all this time his touch still affected her. She'd tried her best over the years to forget her first love, but now circumstances were making it even harder.

"That went well." Jordan hummed an upbeat tune under his breath as they walked. "Don't you think?"

Allie quickly fished a doughnut from the sack and took a big bite, nodding. She handed Jordan the bag, brushing the white powder from her fingers onto a napkin. He obviously hadn't felt the physical spark she'd felt inside Theo's, and it was definitely for the best. Until she convinced herself the past was still in the past, she'd better keep her mouth shut—or risk handing Jordan her heart for a second time.

Jordan walked down Main Street beside Allie, hoping she couldn't hear the heavy pounding of his heart. They'd hit three other businesses since Theo's, and yet his hand still ached to touch her again. The move inside the diner had been purely automatic, and it wasn't until he felt the softness of her sweater that he nearly stumbled over his words. But Allie's tense silence indicated what she thought of his reckless action. Would she bring it up and lecture him on keeping professional distance, or let it go?

Beside him, Allie walked with her head down, fiddling with her gloves. He needed to find a way to break the ice fast, before she decided this job wasn't worth the awkwardness after all and find work elsewhere.

"Jordan?"

Allie's soft voice snapped him back to the present, and Jordan whipped his head to face her. "Yes?"

"Didn't you say we were going into the post office next?" Allie pointed to the doorway he'd walked right past. "Or should we keep going to Greta's Gifts?"

"No, the post office is next. Sorry about that." He reached to open the door, but Allie quickly beat him to it.

"Were you daydreaming about the festival? It seems like we've gotten a good support base so far. Everyone seems excited about participating." They stepped inside the post office, and the official quiet of the lobby wrapped around them like a cozy quilt.

Jordan struggled to keep his mind on Allie's

question and not on the way her plaid scarf made her eyes a darker blue. "I think so, too." Her eyes drew him in, and he took a sharp breath before turning his gaze away.

"You okay?" Allie's voice dipped in concern as she unwound her scarf from her neck. "We probably came out of the cold and into this heat too fast."

Jordan forced what he hoped was a casual smile and nod before motioning for Allie to lead the way to the clerk's counter. What was he getting himself into? Things were getting heated, all right—and it had nothing to do with the temperature inside the post office.

Chapter Five

Allie pulled a homemade Christmas ornament from the plastic tub and winced. "Mom, I can't believe you kept this. It doesn't even look like a reindeer anymore."

Her mother laughed and took the lopsided, wooden decoration from Allie's hand. "You say that every year."

Allie's sister, Molly, draped another layer of tinsel on the bottom branches of the tree. "Wait until you become a parent, Allie. You'll love that stuff. I know Tim and I do." She glanced at her four-year-old daughter, Sophie, who was busy sucking on a candy cane. "It's priceless."

"That's right." Her mother hung the reindeer ornament on a prominent branch. "You'll understand one day."

Allie pulled her knees up to her chest and clasped her arms around them, forcing a smile. Her mother and sister meant well, but it seemed like they were always reminding Allie how she wasn't part of the "mom" club. She hadn't planned on being twenty-eight and single. Once upon a time, she'd imagined herself decorating a Christmas tree with several of her own children helping out.

"Who wants cocoa?" Her father's voice boomed as he appeared in the doorway, holding a tray laden with goodies.

"Me!" Sophie sprung up, abandoning her sticky candy cane. "With marshmallows!"

Her mother took the tray and passed out steaming mugs. Molly sat down with Sophie in her lap and showed her how to blow on the hot chocolate to cool it off. "Isn't this nice?' her mother said. "All of us together for Christmas again. Well, except for Tim, but he'll be here later, right, Molly?"

As her sister nodded, Allie's head throbbed with sudden repressed tears, and she stood. "It's getting hot in here. I'm going to take my cocoa on the porch."

"Everything all right?" Her mother's brows arched. "I can turn the heater down."

"No, it's okay. I'll be right back." Allie hurried out the front door before anyone could argue.

The night wind caressed Allie's face as she settled into one of the white rockers and pushed off with her feet. She swayed back and forth with the breeze, grateful for the cool air that took the edge off her frustration. If she ever wanted to be a real member of the family, she'd have to be married—like Molly. Have a child—like Molly. Be successful—like Molly. How many times had their mother mentioned Molly's catering business in the past three days?

Allie closed her eyes, trying to clear her mind of her failures and focus on the tree frogs' night-time chorus instead. She'd forgotten how peaceful and calming country life was—like a balm to her soul. Her old apartment in Kansas City bounced with activity and constant noise—music from the neighbors' teenagers, dogs barking, car horns honking.

Headlights swept across the porch as an SUV pulled into the long drive. Allie planted her feet to stop the rocking with a jerk. Who would be out in her parents' neck of the woods this late in the evening? The driver's door opened, and a tall, trim figure stepped outside. Dark shadows hid his identity, and his footsteps crunched the snow as he made his way toward the path. Allie hesitated, not sure if she should call for her father or demand to know the stranger's name.

Before she could decide, the porch light illuminated Jordan's face. Allie stood as he easily scaled the porch stairs. "What are you doing here?"

"You left your scarf in the office." Jordan held up the plaid scarf Allie had worn to work that morning. "I thought you might need it tomorrow."

"Thanks." Allie took the long swatch of fabric

from him and draped it around her neck. "You didn't have to bring it all the way out here. I could have gotten it tomorrow."

"I didn't mind the drive. It's a nice night. Besides, I don't think I've been here since the pregraduation party your family hosted for our senior class." Jordan shoved his hands in his jacket pocket and rocked back on his heels. He glanced around the house with a smile. "Looks like not much has changed."

Allie cleared her throat. "It's been nearly a decade. You must have a great head for directions if you remembered how to get here."

Jordan lifted one shoulder in a shrug. "My car has a GPS."

"Oh. Right." So he didn't remember after all. Allie shoved aside her disappointment and dared to glance into his eyes. Still deep chocolate-brown, with the lethal capability to melt her like a Hershey's bar. She looked away before her emotions surpassed her good judgment. It didn't matter what she felt. She was only here for a few weeks, then she'd be back where the protests of her heart could be safely drowned out by the noise of Kansas City. Back where she could hopefully throw herself into a new business and really show her family what she was capable of—with or without a man.

"Would you like to come in?" Allie straightened

her spine, determined not to show her vulnerability. Just because they weren't at work didn't mean she had to lose her professionalism. It was the only way she'd survive these few weeks.

"Actually, I'd like to talk out here, if that's all right." Jordan rested his weight against the porch railing and crossed his arms over his chest. A hint of a rust-colored sweater peeked beneath the dark leather of his jacket, and Allie remembered all those times during high school football games that she'd buried herself under the soft folds of his coat and snuggled into his embrace. She shivered imagining his warmth.

"Are you cold? I'm sorry. Here I am keeping you outside, and you don't even have a coat." Jordan pulled off his jacket and draped it around her shoulders before Allie could protest.

It smelled like his spicy cologne—and the past. The porch reeled with the sudden onslaught of memories, and Allie clutched the jacket around her, desperate to hold on to the good times. Jordan, grinning at her from the driver's seat of his beat-up Camaro as she slid in for a date. She and Jordan, snuggled together on the bench of the gazebo on Main Street, pretending it was much colder outside than it was. Jordan, racing around the track at a meet and blowing her a kiss from the finish line.

Then the happy recollections faded into grim

reality. Jordan, ignoring her e-mails the month before Christmas break. Jordan, putting off her phone calls. Jordan, daring to break her heart at their special spot inside the town's gazebo.

A sudden wave of anger burned through Allie, and she shoved the jacket back into his arms. "You know, I'm suddenly not feeling very well." It wasn't a lie. She'd never felt more nauseous in her life.

Jordan frowned with surprise. "I'm sorry, was it something—"

"I'm fine. It's nothing. I'll see you at work tomorrow, okay?" She flashed a quick smile in his direction, averting her eyes to hide the tears pooling within, and reached for the doorknob. *Please, just go. Don't make me be rude.* She drew a deep breath, determined to calm down and not let him see her pain, despite the emotions welling inside.

Jordan's confused expression lingered in front of her as he murmured a surprised agreement. "Of course. Tomorrow, then."

She wrenched the knob with more force than necessary, offering a quick wave and shutting the door against his well wishes. She pressed a hand to her stomach as she planted her back against the closed door and slid to a sitting position. Tomorrow. And the day after that. And the day after that. She pushed her fingers against her pounding temples.

Then she realized she still had no idea what Jordan had wanted to talk about.

* * *

Jordan winced as the front door shut tightly against its frame. He looked at his coat and then back at the house as if either object could give him an answer.

He'd come over to give Allie the scarf, hoping she wouldn't see through the flimsy excuse and into his desire just to be near her. They'd been apart not even three hours this evening when he realized how much he missed her smile. Her laugh. Her kind words.

All of which, unfortunately, had been directed at various vendors of Ginger Falls today and not at him.

Jordan slipped his arms back into the sleeves of his coat, then jerked as the front door squeaked open again. An older, blond version of Allie stepped outside, one hand clutching a little girl's arm. She looked up in surprise. "Oh! I'm sorry, I didn't hear anyone knock." She glanced back toward the house and then at Jordan. "Who are you?"

She didn't remember him. It was not surprising, as Molly had been in college when he and Allie dated. "I'm Jordan, Allie's ex—I mean, her friend. No, her boss." Jordan held out his hand with a sheepish smile. "Hi. I'm Jordan."

"Molly, Allie's sister. And this is Sophie." Molly ruffled the child's hair. "We were about to head home for the night. Do you want me to get Allie for you?"

"No, that's okay. We already talked. I was just leaving."

Confusion puzzled Molly's eyes. "Okay, if you're sure. Good night, then." She waved as they started down the stairs, and Sophie did the same, her smile coated with what looked like chocolate stains. Jordan's heart softened at the sight. He'd always wanted kids of his own one day. He had always pictured them with a mop of Allie's curly hair and his own dark eyes.

But those pictures had long since faded.

Molly hesitated on the bottom step. "Wait. Jordan…Jordan Walker?"

"That's me." Jordan lifted both arms in a shrug.

"I get it now." Molly smirked before opening the door to her car. "If I were you, I wouldn't hold my breath out here, if you know what I mean."

"Don't worry, she's my employee now, nothing more." Unfortunately. After her quick exit just now, he probably stood a better chance at catching a star than becoming Allie's friend again.

He made his way toward his own SUV, waving goodbye to Sophie as Molly secured the child in her booster seat. Nothing like going home on a cold night with only a reality check for company. He pulled his keys from his pocket. It was his own fault. He should've realized what he'd had ten years ago and not wasted so much time trying to please other people.

"Jordan?"

He turned silently at Molly's call.

She grinned before sliding behind the steering wheel. "On second thought, it might be a good idea to hold that breath just a little while longer." She gestured toward the house.

Jordan followed her pointing finger with his eyes just in time to see the lacy front curtain fall back into place.

Chapter Six

"I can't believe Christmas is less than one week away." Allie adjusted the dark green cloth on the card table so it hung straight on both sides. She'd been in Ginger Falls for almost two weeks. Now it was Sunday afternoon, and the festival they'd been working toward all this time would start tomorrow.

"I know. Everything is really coming together. Did you fax those reminder flyers to the list of businesses I gave you?" Jordan popped out the legs of the second table and swung it into position. The clatter echoed against the gym walls. The local high school had given their permission to host the first event in the gym, so there would be plenty of space for everyone during the contest.

"Yes, and I received confirmations from all of them. I did that Friday—before I knew you'd have me working on a Sunday afternoon." Allie scrunched her nose at Jordan.

He laughed, and the deep timbre shivered up her spine. Allie quickly reached down for the bag of fake snow and began to spread the glittery cotton over the tablecloth. She'd learned over the past several days how to distract herself every time her emotions threatened to take over. Better to ignore her growing feelings for Jordan than to follow her heart's instinct and plant a big kiss on the five o'clock shadow he couldn't seem to keep off his cheeks, regardless of the time of day.

"I normally would never ask an employee to work on a Sunday." Jordan stepped back from the tables lining the back wall and studied them before continuing. "But the gingerbread bake-off starts so early in the morning that it'd be impossible to get everything set up before then. We'll be done in plenty of time for you to make it back to the evening service, if that was your plan."

"Are you going?" Allie hoped he didn't think the question was an invitation. It was more of a security measure. If he was, she'd rather camp out in the guest room at her parents' house and study her Bible alone than sit by Jordan in a pew again. That Sunday morning had been brutal. She'd been sitting on the end of the row beside her father when Jordan slipped inside the back of the church and whispered for her to move down. She'd had no choice but to comply and spent the rest of the service trying to make sure their elbows didn't brush for fear of a chemistry fire.

"I'd like to." He flashed a bright smile. "What about you?"

Allie shrugged and focused on the snow arrangement she was creating. Her conscience pricked at how she'd practically thrown his jacket at him the other night, and she stole at glance at Jordan's broad back as he lifted a giant gingerbread cutout onto the center of one of the tables. She realized she didn't know what she wanted anymore, other than peace.

And being around Jordan was the most chaos her heart had experienced in a long time.

For the first time in his professional life, Jordan felt nervous. He ran a hand through his hair, forgetting he'd carefully styled it that morning for the big event, and paced the front of the gym. The gingerbread bake-off was scheduled to start within the half hour, and so far, the room was empty, save for Allie and a handful of high school volunteers, off school for winter break. What if no one showed up? What if all their advertising was for naught? What if he failed miserably in his goal to restore Ginger Falls—not only its finances, but its heart?

To his right, Allie hunched over one of the tables, carefully adjusting the gingerbread house they'd pieced together at work on Friday. She'd been so adorable, her nose wrinkled in concentration as she glued together gingerbread walls with thick icing. They'd worked together great that next week, but Allie was still keeping a distance that belied their once-close friendship. Maybe it was for the best. After all, she reminded him almost daily how she couldn't wait to get back to Kansas City.

"You all right?" Allie made her way over to Jordan, brushing glitter from the table off the front of her dress pants. She'd traded her typical casual work attire for black slacks and a powder-blue top that made her eyes even bluer.

"Just worried if this event will be a success or not." He glanced over his shoulder toward the gym door, which was propped open to encourage passersby to stop in. "I'm a little concerned that no one is here yet."

"We did a lot of advertising and received good feedback from the surrounding communities. I think you can relax." Allie patted his arm, then snatched her hand back, feeling her cheeks go red. "I better go check on the food Theo brought." She scurried across the gym, leaving Jordan with an imprint on his forearm and a warmth in his stomach that had nothing to do with his nerves.

You are such a glutton for punishment. Allie berated herself the entire way to the snack table. She forced a smile at Theo, the diner owner, who was scooping ice into plastic cups. "Anything you need here?"

"Nope, we're all set. I'll head back to the diner in a few minutes, after I finish this." Theo waved the ice scooper. "Thank you kindly."

"No problem." Allie turned slowly, wishing she had something productive to do to stay busy—in other words, to avoid Jordan. He looked so jittery. She had to admit she felt the same—just not for the same reasons. *God, please help me to focus on the event today and not mess things up. You know how good I am at that lately.*

A group of middle-aged women strode into the gym, each carrying a platter full of gingerbread. Her mother and Molly were right behind them, their contest entries covered in aluminum foil. Allie let out a slow breath as more people filed inside the gym, including Mayor Cubley and his committee, as well as Greta from the gift shop on Main Street. Looks like they'd have some participation today after all. She glanced at Jordan, who deflated with relief.

Allie hurried over to the group to begin assigning numbers to the gingerbread entries and marking places on the table. There was no time to worry—about Jordan or her family. She had a town to save.

And a heart to protect.

"I'm never eating gingerbread again." Allie lay on the gym floor with her arms sprawled to the sides.

Beside her, Jordan stood, arms crossed as he looked down at her prone figure with a knowing smirk. If she had the energy, she'd kick him. But that would require moving. After being so busy, she had zero energy.

"No one told you to sample a piece of every entry. You weren't even a judge." Jordan eased into a sitting position beside her on the hardwood floor. "You do know this floor is filthy?"

"I don't care." Allie moaned. "Is all the gingerbread gone?"

Jordan looked toward the back of the gym where the high school volunteers were taking down the tables. "Looks like it. Mostly due to you."

She laughed as she struggled upright. "You can't blame me for participating. Besides, I saw you carrying around at least three big pieces of that ginger-raisin loaf earlier."

"Touché." Jordan offered a hand to help, but Allie ignored it. She wasn't about to ignite another spark between them.

She rested her weight on her palms, her legs stretched in front of her. "I never want to see gingerbread again. Or smell it."

"Don't be so sure you can escape that easily. I saw your sister's muffins won first place." Jordan smiled. "I'm sure there's plenty more where that came from."

Allie's mood sank to join the rock in her stomach.

Of course her ideal wife, mother-of-the-year sister would win. Their parents had been so wrapped up in Molly's victory that they hadn't even said goodbye when they left with her mini trophy.

"All in all, I'd say today was a big success. I heard several people mention they were bringing their families to tomorrow's event." Jordan stood and brushed at his slacks.

Allie reluctantly did the same, trying to press the negative thoughts of her family aside. "The forecast predicts snow tonight, which would give everyone a great base for the snowman building contest tomorrow morning."

"Snow *gingerbread* man," Jordan corrected.

"Ugh, you had to say the *G*-word." Allie clutched her stomach.

"Come on, you." Jordan slung his arm around Allie's shoulders and propelled her toward the gym door. "We've got work to do for tomorrow."

"Does that include a nap?" Allie tried to keep her tone light and playful but heard the quiver in her voice. Would Jordan's touch ever cease to affect her? Did he feel the same way at all?

"If we get everything done, then you can get off work at 3:30 instead of 5:00. Deal?" Jordan's arm dropped from around her as he opened the door for them to exit.

Allie stepped outside, squinting against the brightness. The noon sun warmed her skin—but the absence of Jordan's embrace chilled her to the core. She closed her eyes and shivered. "Deal."

Chapter Seven

A snowball slid, wet and cold, down the neck of Jordan's sweater. "Hey!" He spun around, searching for the culprit. Children in bright ski jackets rolled balls of snow against the icy front yard of the high school, packing them into place with the help of their parents. The more experienced crafters meticulously carved designs into their snowman creations with ice picks and colored dye. No one looked as if they'd just launched an icy attack.

A snort sounded from his left. He turned to see Allie attempting to cover a laugh with her gloved hand.

"Very subtle." Jordan walked slowly toward her, pausing to scoop a handful of snow from the ground. He rolled it between his hands as he neared her spot by a tree. "You do realize I'm still your boss?"

Allie ducked, covering her face with her arms. "Maybe I didn't think this one through."

"I'll say." Jordan aimed the snowball with a grin. Allie squealed and ran. Jordan made a quick maneuver to head her off, but his legs slipped out from under him. He fell, one foot accidentally tripping up Allie's escape. She crashed to the ground beside him with a shriek.

Jordan rolled to his side. "Are you okay?"

"I think so." Allie swiped snow from her face and laughed. "But I'm starting to realize the original snowball wasn't worth it." She sat up.

Jordan grinned as he pulled himself into a sitting position beside her. "You've got snow in your hair." He pulled off his glove and gently brushed at the ice clinging to her curls. His fingers tangled in the dark strands.

Allie's gaze met his, vulnerable and open for the first time since she came back into his life. They stared at each other. The chatter and laughter of the contestants around them faded until all Jordan could hear was the heavy thumping of his heart. He forced his gaze away from her mouth, trying not to wonder… He swallowed against his dry throat. "Allie, I—"

"There you are!" Mayor Cubley ambled toward them, holding a camera. A wide grin was stretched across his full cheeks. "The judges had a few questions for you two before they begin the scoring process."

Jordan looked back at Allie. The expression in

her eyes hovered between relief and disappointment, mirroring the feeling in his own gut. He nodded at the mayor as he stood, pulling Allie up with him. "No problem, Mayor."

"Let's get a quick shot of the brainpower behind the return of the Gingerbread Festival." Mayor Cubley raised his camera. "Everybody say snowman!"

Jordan forced a smile and looped a casual arm around Allie's shoulder for the picture. Talk about bad timing. He'd been close to kissing her, but such a move would have surely been the final nail in their coffin. How could he win back her trust and friendship if she thought he was coming on to her? Then again, there had been a look of disappointment in her eyes. Had he only imagined it? Would Allie want his kiss after all this time? He'd done nothing to earn it.

They followed the mayor toward the table of judges, who pointed at clipboards and gestured to the surrounding gingerbread-snowmen. Jordan drew a deep breath of frigid air and tried to focus on the judges.

He'd never know now.

Allie stared numbly at the rows of gaily decorated gingerbread-snowmen, vaguely aware of the judge's questions being asked of her. Jordan answered each one, but the words wouldn't compute. All she could think about was the unspoken message in Jordan's eyes when he'd gently cradled her face with his hand. Even though his fingers had been cold, heat had warmed her all the way to her boot-clad feet. For a moment, she thought he would kiss her.

And for an even briefer moment, she'd wanted him to.

The judges began to announce the contest winners, and a young child and his dad slapped a high five at their victory. Allie smiled as she handed the duo a small trophy, donated by a local store. The community had really rallied around the week's events, and from the grin on Jordan's face as he congratulated the winners and runners-up, he realized it, too. Maybe now he could relax and drop his concerns about the townspeople not participating.

Allie waved at her niece, Sophie, and her brother-in-law, Tim, who stood by their lopsided creation a few entries down the line. They hadn't even placed, but Sophie didn't seem to care as she proudly snapped a picture of their snowman.

Allie's smile wavered. What would it be like to one day participate in the Gingerbread Festival with her own children? She'd been so focused on her career these past few years. Was it worth it? She swallowed the lump in her throat. Her mother and Molly certainly seemed happy. But then again, she thought she had been, too—until she'd lost her job.

And Jordan walked back into her life.

Confusion swirled like the snowflakes that stirred

the ground, and Allie lifted her face to the gray, overcast sky. But any answer remained locked in the clouds.

"What are you doing out here alone?" Molly's voice rose above the wind as Allie trudged through the snow, toward the trails leading to the Christmas trees. "It's almost dark."

Allie clicked on her flashlight. "Just needed some fresh air."

Molly walked toward her, hands shoved into the front pockets of her red peacoat. "You sure do require a lot of air lately." She joined Allie on the path and looked up. "It is a nice night, though."

Allie followed her gaze. The clouds from earlier in the day had drifted, leaving a clear sky that quickly faded to dusk. Remnants of hot pink and orange still painted the horizon. She let out a slow breath and started walking. "Fresh air is code for thinking."

Molly fell into step beside her. "About Jordan?"

Allie hesitated a beat. "How'd you know?"

"We're sisters." Molly playfully hip-bumped her in the side. "I always knew about your crushes growing up. Besides, you didn't make it that hard—you kept your journal under your mattress for the world to find."

"I thought *younger* sisters were supposed to be the snoops."

Molly shrugged. "I was bored. We lived in the

middle of nowhere." She gestured to the green expanse of trees around them.

"Well, you got over that quick." Allie's voice sobered. "Now you have the perfect life. You're probably never bored."

Molly snorted. "You're half-right. I'm rarely bored, but my life is far from perfect."

Beside them, a squirrel ran down a tree. Allie flicked the light farther down the path. "How is that possible? You have a husband, a family, a successful business." Not for the first time, jealousy raked its nails across Allie's back.

"Every gift comes with struggles." Molly kicked at a pinecone. "Business is good, but it's also stressful because of how busy I stay. And of course I love Tim, but we have our disagreements like every couple." She sighed. "And Sophie is the best thing that ever happened to us, but again, there are rough days—days when I wonder if I'm fit to be a mom."

"You've got to be kidding." Allie stopped walking, the flashlight hanging limp at her side. "You've always had it all together—like superwoman. Even as kids, you were the one with the straight A's, the athletic ability, the popular crowd. You're the last person who should have self-esteem issues."

"I wish." Molly snorted. "Do you seriously believe that I—or anyone else—has it better than you? I know losing your job had to be hard, but you didn't hit rock bottom, Al. You had a safety net. Most people in your position would kill for that kind of padding."

Molly was right. If it hadn't been for her parents letting her live with them temporarily—for free, no less—she'd have been in real trouble. Yet instead of showing her appreciation, she'd been walking around expecting others to voice the disappointment she felt in her own heart.

"You got quiet." Molly started walking again, her boots shuffling against the snow. "Did I say too much?"

"No, just enough." Allie shook her head. "Something to think about, Mol. Thanks." Molly was right. She was very blessed, and her faith should be stronger than this. Growing up, she'd always believed everything happened for a reason; yet for the first time in her life, she was expected to live out that faith, and she'd faltered. What did that say about her?

Allie fought to draw a deep breath. She focused her attention on the deepening shadows of the evening sky instead. Twinkling stars were just beginning to poke through a velvet backdrop, and the wind rustled the tops of the trees, branches silhouetted against the night. The breeze chilled her cheeks, and she pressed her gloved hands against them for warmth.

"So, tell me about Jordan. Is it difficult working with him?" Molly's voice cut the stillness.

"A little." It felt good to admit the truth out loud. "But it's a job, and I like the work. Besides, I'll be going back to Kansas City eventually." She swallowed. "I can handle temporary."

Molly paused. "I think he still has feelings for you."

"What?" Allie stopped short on the path, snow crunching under her boots. "That's crazy." Jordan had been very professional in their weeks together, though the last few days he'd made more of an effort toward friendship. They worked in close quarters and for a common goal. All work and no play would get old fast. That's all it was.

Then again, there had been that almost-kiss at the snowman competition—if she hadn't imagined it.

"Not crazy at all. It's pretty obvious the way he looks at you and the way he hung around the porch that night after dropping off your scarf." Molly pointed the flashlight at Allie and grinned. "And I think you might just feel the same way about him, too."

Allie batted the light away. "Trust me, Molly, that ship has sailed and sunk. Besides, Jordan was the one who broke up with me. I doubt he's changed his mind in the last decade." The fact coated her insides with a chill much deeper than the one teasing her skin through her coat. She might have left Jordan on the porch the other week, but he'd left her in the cold first. She snatched the flashlight from her sister and shone it on the path. "Come on, let's go inside."

Molly smirked, then turned to lead the way. Her words floated over her shoulder and straight into Allie's heart. "All right, but your face says it all, Allie—in letters just as big and bold as your old journal entries."

Chapter Eight

"Good news." Jordan sat back in his office desk chair with a loud squeak of leather. "I counted up the guests' donations last night with Mayor Cubley after you left the snowman contest, and we've already raised significant funds just from the first two events."

"That's great." Across the desk on the floor, Allie looked up briefly from the banner she was making for that night's competition and smiled. "Every little bit will help." She pressed a cutout gingerbread man onto the banner, testing to see if the glue would stick to the canvas. It felt good to forget her own struggles temporarily and invest her energy into something tangible and worthwhile like this community program. Taking the job of Jordan's assistant had proven good for Allie in ways deeper than just a paycheck— though she had to admit she was looking forward to Christmas shopping this week.

"That's not all," Jordan continued. "According to the mayor, several shop owners in nearby cities have seen our advertising for the big Christmas Eve finale and love the idea. They've even inquired about leasing store space here. They think Ginger Falls is charming and want in before all the good property is gone." He grinned mischievously. "Of course, I didn't tell them it would take quite a while to fill up all the free spaces."

Allie shook her head in amazement. "All because of a gingerbread bake-off and a snowman contest?" Who would have thought they'd be this successful this fast?

"It's not because of the events. It's because of the heart of the city." Jordan leaned forward, seemingly unable to contain his excitement. "They can see what we're all about here in Ginger Falls—and they want to be a part of it." He slapped the desk with one hand and beamed. "Isn't that great?"

"You're really passionate about this, aren't you?" Allie set down the bottle of glue and studied Jordan, the light in his eyes, the flush in his face as he talked. Maybe that was her problem. Allie had enjoyed the bookstore she'd worked at, had liked being around books all day and assisting customers. It'd been fulfilling—but it had never stirred inside her what obviously stirred inside Jordan. Was passion the missing ingredient for success?

"It's what I've wanted for years, ever since I

came back to visit and saw how much the city had changed." He sobered. "It just didn't seem right. California was a real eye-opener to my priorities—taught me the importance of slowing down and appreciating the little things." His gaze pierced hers as she looked up. "And the value of second chances."

Allie picked up the scissors and cut out another star, trying not to extract any extra meaning from Jordan's gaze. She fought to keep her voice steady despite her trembling fingers. "Ginger Falls certainly deserves a second chance."

"Right. Ginger Falls." Jordan's voice trailed off.

She glued the last star and lifted both arms in a stretch, hoping Jordan couldn't hear her heart pounding from across the room. Of course he couldn't possibly have been talking about their relationship. Molly's little speech last night must have put crazy ideas in her head—and that was the last thing her heart needed. "I think that's it for this one."

Jordan stood and peered over the desk. "Wow. I had no idea I hired an artist when I hired an assistant."

"Hardly." Allie wrinkled her nose as she studied the banner. Glittery stars, gingerbread men and green and red candies decorated the white background. Bold letters in the middle spelled out the details for that afternoon's gingerbread man cookie-decorating contest.

"You're too modest." Jordan came around to her

spot on the floor and offered a hand to help her up. "You're very talented, Allie. You've been a great help around here these few weeks we've been together."

She accepted his offer and stood, ignoring how wonderful the word *together* sounded on his lips. She avoided meeting his eyes as she tugged her hand free. If she looked up now, she'd inevitably invite that near-kiss from yesterday, and that would be nothing but a disaster.

An amazing, wonderful, perfect disaster but a disaster all the same.

"We'd better head over to Main Street and get this banner hung. There's only three hours until the event." She stepped away from Jordan and stared at the canvas on the floor, hoping he didn't notice the tremble in her voice. She struggled to keep her mind on the upcoming tasks. "Were all the toppings donated as we requested, or should we run through the grocery store first?"

Jordan squatted down and carefully began to roll up the banner. "Theo and some of the others from the diner said they had it covered. Gumdrops, icing, licorice, sprinkles and jelly beans, right?"

Allie nodded slowly. She debated helping Jordan roll the banner, but then she'd be near him again, their heads close together, hands nearly touching as they met in the middle at the canvas. No. Definitely not. She busied herself with throwing on her coat instead, taking her time with her scarf.

"Theo said yesterday that his business has boomed so much over the last two days from guests attending the festival that he's nearly doubled his profits, even after deducting the costs of his donations." Jordan stood, the banner tucked under his arm. "Things are really moving along."

"Right on schedule." Allie forced a smile as she quickly collected the string and scissors with which to tie the banner. Things were moving along all right, including her time in Ginger Falls. If her requested loan didn't come through, what would she do? Could she really be happy staying in Ginger Falls, living with her parents or in a small apartment, working for Jordan? Would there be enough work for her to do after the holidays to keep her employed? She'd probably have to find another job and try to save enough cash to move back to Kansas City.

Then *she'd* be the one leaving Jordan in her dust.

Allie stuffed the supplies in her purse and allowed Jordan to open the office door for her, reminding him to lock it behind them as they headed for the elevator. She studied his chiseled jaw and dark hair as they waited in the hallway for the elevator. He whistled under his breath, the banner tucked under one arm, the other hand slung casually in his jacket pocket. He was even more handsome than he'd been the last time she'd seen him, a freshman in college.

She looked away before he could catch her stare.

Before, the thought of leaving brought comfort to her bruised ego. It would serve Jordan right for her to leave and never look back like he'd done to her ten years ago.

But for some reason now, it only brought a heavy cloud of disappointment.

Jordan breathed a sigh of relief as he surveyed the contest going on before him. Another great turnout. Even the sun was shining this late afternoon, providing an extra bit of warmth for the eager children. A dozen tables full of kids and their parents filled the north end of Main Street, a plethora of brightly colored hats, jackets and scarves. The banner Allie had created was draped across the front of the dilapidated gazebo behind them, a cheerful contradiction to the gloomy, weakened structure. Three events down, two to go. That is, if they were able to pull off the big Christmas Eve finale.

"Jordan!" Mayor Cubley strode across the street, his trademark loafers leaving shadowed patches in the melted snow. "Great news, son. We've received permission to use Leonard Mitchell's pasture for the festival finale. He said he could put his horses in another field for the night."

"Great." Jordan breathed a relieved sigh. "I was getting concerned about the location. We've advertised everything but where. I'll have Allie make up some new signs with the details."

"Everything still on with the pilot?"

"Yes, sir. We're good to go. We'll start the event off here on Main Street, then meet at Leonard's field at seven o'clock for the picture. Probably wouldn't hurt to offer a bus to help shuttle folks, so we don't have cars parked all over Leonard's farm. Then everyone can come back to Main Street afterward for the carriage rides."

"No problem. I'll handle the bus." The mayor pulled a notepad from his shirt pocket and scribbled on the page. "This is shaping up to be a grand event," he said with a smile.

"I think so, too." Jordan turned to survey the rows of children busily decorating their cookies. He couldn't help but laugh at Allie's niece, Sophie, who had more icing on her face than on her cookie. The little girl bent carefully over her project, cheeks stuffed with gumdrops.

Mayor Cubley followed his gaze with a chuckle. "She's quite the little artist."

"Just like her aunt." Jordan glanced around the square for Allie, who had vanished after helping him set up the event. Come to think of it, she said she'd been going to get hot chocolate, and that'd been almost an hour ago.

Jordan patted the mayor's shoulder. "Mayor, I'm going to find Allie and talk business for a bit. I'll catch you later."

"Of course. You two remember to have some fun,

now, you hear?" The mayor lowered his voice to a gruff warning, but the twinkle in his eyes belied the tone.

"Yes, sir." Jordan waved and headed toward the refreshment table, set up by the curb on Main Street. There was no sign of Allie, but her sister Molly stood beside the large thermos of hot chocolate, pouring the liquid into a paper cup.

"Hi, there." She waved as he drew near. "Great crowd today! How are things going so far?"

"Very well." Jordan plucked a cup from the stack and helped himself.

"Are you a judge?"

"No, thank goodness." Jordan dropped a few marshmallows into his cocoa. "It'd be hard to decide. I figure since I'm the program director I should remain a neutral party."

"So I guess I can't bribe you to vote for Sophie." Molly laughed.

"If she keeps up at her current rate, she could win best decorated child, instead of cookie."

Molly shook her head. "I better go play referee, then. I got her a cup of hot chocolate, but I'm guessing she's already sugared out."

"Have you seen Allie lately? I lost her in the crowd."

"No. Actually, I haven't seen her at all today." Molly frowned. "Is everything okay?"

"I hope so. She was fine at work this afternoon.

Did you see her banner?" Jordan gestured to the gazebo, where the advertisement hung. "She made it herself. Nice job, huh?"

Molly's eyes darted to the colored canvas, and understanding dawned on her face. "This is the first event that's been on Main Street this week, isn't it?"

"Yeah, the first two were at the high school." Jordan shrugged. "Why?" He followed Molly's steady gaze, but the banner, now flapping slightly in the breeze, didn't reveal the same secret.

Molly tossed her empty cup into the trash beside the refreshment table. "Don't tell me you don't remember."

"Remember what?" What was the problem with Main Street? He frowned, looking back at the banner, then it hit him.

The gazebo.

The spot where he met Allie nearly a decade ago, during their first holiday break from college—the spot where he'd ended their relationship on Christmas Eve. He winced, his gaze jumping from the broken bench on the platform to the crooked steps, one dangling by a few nails. The structure obviously still held bad memories for Allie.

Funny—he could only remember the good ones.

Chapter Nine

Allie snuck down the stairs into the living room, sucking in her breath at the squeaky third step. She felt like a teenager again, tiptoeing around after curfew. Tonight, though, she was hoping to remain incognito for a different reason. Christmas Eve was two days away, and she had yet to enjoy her favorite tradition—even if she was a little embarrassed to admit she still looked forward to it every year.

But after the day she'd had, Allie needed all the holiday spirit she could stand.

She stumbled through the dark into the living room, fumbling around the floor by the wall for the extension cord. She found the little switch and pushed. The tree lit up, a soft glow that pressed away the deep shadows of the night.

With a quick glance at the empty staircase, Allie lay flat on the floor on her back and scooted until she was halfway under the tree, looking up through the sage-colored branches into the expanse of twinkling lights. Candy canes and red garland nestled against the limbs, while a variety of ornaments—store-bought and homemade—dangled amid the greenery. Allie narrowed her eyes to a squint, the golden lights now a shiny, twisting blur against the darkness. She breathed deeply of the evergreen scent and slowly released her breath, feeling relaxed for the first time in weeks.

Finally, the embrace of Christmas.

She hadn't thought the gazebo would wrench her back in time the way it did. After all, she'd paid her dues to the structure when she first arrived back in town weeks ago. But standing beside Jordan at the very site where he'd broken her heart had been more than she could handle. She'd helped him hang the banner and kept her emotions in check, then made an excuse about getting a snack and carefully avoided him the rest of the event. She stayed to the background, making sure the hot chocolate kept flowing and the marshmallows didn't run out. But despite Jordan's obvious attempts at looking for her, she hadn't been in the mood to talk with him again. If she was going to finish her job these next few weeks, she had to keep him at a distance. Seeing compassion—or worse, pity—in his eyes at her tears would have done her in.

Allie shifted on the tree skirt, trying to find a more comfortable place. Molly was wrong. Jordan didn't still care for her the way he once did. If anything, he was just trying to be a friend. It wasn't his fault her stubborn memories and feelings kept her locked in the past every time she was near him.

A thump sounded by the stairs. Allie jerked up, tree needles poking into her cheeks. "Ow!"

"Allie, is that you?" Her mother's figure appeared by the tree. She knotted the belt of her robe and bent to peer beneath the greenery. "What are you doing down there?"

"Getting assaulted by tree branches." Allie rubbed the sting on her forehead. So much for a peaceful break from reality. She started to pull herself out but stopped in surprise as her mother lowered herself to the floor.

Mom awkwardly wiggled her way under the branches beside Allie. "I remember the first time I saw you do this as a child." She laughed.

Allie moved her head to give her mother more room, careful not to knock against the hard metal stand. "You all thought I was crazy." It hadn't been the first time Allie felt left out while she was growing up, and at this rate, she was pretty much guaranteed it wouldn't be the last.

"Your sister thought you were nuts, that's for sure." Her mother laughed again. "But I thought it was creative. I always wondered what you saw under here that none of us did." She angled her neck and peered through the branches as if searching for the secret.

"That's easy." Allie smiled. "I saw Christmas."

"You know, you were—and are—a bright girl, Allie." Her mom released a long breath. "I just don't know why you always seemed drawn to take the hard path."

A defensive bubble formed in Allie's chest. "Easy isn't always right."

"That's true. But at the same time, neither is the opposite. Life doesn't always *have* to be difficult, the way you tend to make it."

The easy camaraderie vanished beneath the tree, and Allie struggled to take a breath against the sudden weight on her chest. Here it came—the conversation her mother had obviously wanted to have ever since Allie's arrival weeks ago. "We're talking about my old job again, aren't we?"

"If you'd taken the job we'd hoped you would after graduating, this wouldn't have happened." She twisted her head toward Allie, but Allie kept her gaze riveted to the tree.

She swallowed hard. "I know, Mom. But there's something to be said for taking risks. Look at Jordan, for example. He loves this town so much that he was willing to invest his own finances in order to bring it back to the way it was before. Without him taking that risk, the entire town would be negatively affected."

"You're right. But not everyone is cut out to take those kinds of risks."

"Was it not a risk for Molly to start a catering business?" Allie looked over at her mother. "How is that any different than my choice to pursue a career I was actually interested in? To pursue my dream of owning a bookstore?"

"Molly is older, settled. She's married. She's got a savings account and a fallback plan." Her mother's eyes pleaded with Allie. "Why don't you get settled before you move back to Kansas City with these lofty dreams?"

Allie clenched her fists as her frustration boiled over. Why couldn't her mother just love her for who she was instead of for what she did? Allie would never be Molly. Would her family ever accept that? "That's not possible." She couldn't stay indefinitely, even if she wanted to.

Not with Jordan in the same town.

Ironic that ten years ago, Jordan's absence helped push Allie away from Ginger Falls. Now, his presence was accomplishing the exact same goal.

"Why not? Maybe you could even date Jordan again—all that stuff between you two was ages ago." Her mother's hand waved through the air in dismissal, almost knocking a penguin ornament off its branch. "I knew if I told you Jordan was the program director that you'd never have accepted the position the job agency offered."

"You knew it was Jordan and didn't warn me? How could you?"

"It was no big deal. You just needed a little push." Her mom spun a toy top on a string, and the ornament bobbed against the branches.

"Let me ask you this—did you *push* Molly into her marriage, or was she capable of finding love on her own?" Allie edged out from under the tree. She couldn't stay there and ruin her favorite holiday tradition any longer. This was exactly why she'd had to leave Ginger Falls in the first place. Her family hadn't supported her goals then, and they didn't now.

Her mother sat up, adjusting her robe as Allie hurried toward the staircase. "You don't understand. I just want you to—"

"No, Mom. Trust me. I totally understand." Allie hesitated at the bottom of the staircase, fighting back another rush of burning tears. "Thanks for believing in me." She rushed up the stairs, leaving her mother alone on the living room floor.

The clinking of forks on plates and the low murmurs of patrons seemed nearly deafening in the silent tension that stretched across the chipped table. Jordan shut his laptop with a snap. "Okay, what's going on?"

From the other side of the booth, Allie looked up from her plate with a start. "What do you mean?"

"I mean, you've barely spoken three words since we sat down, and you haven't touched your food.

Theo's Morning Bird special is one of the best breakfast combos I've ever had." Jordan gestured to Allie's plate, still full of eggs, bacon and grits. "Something must be wrong." *Just please don't let it be something I did.* His silent prayer drifted through the smoky haze of the diner, and he held his breath. He purposefully hadn't pushed the issue of Allie's absence yesterday at the cookie contest, choosing to hope that she'd trust him and share her feelings first.

Allie set down the fork she'd been twirling between her fingers. "It's hard to eat on a full stomach."

Jordan frowned. "You ate before coming to a breakfast meeting?" He'd asked Allie to meet him early for work, before the next festival event began later in the afternoon. He wanted to go over some figures and finish planning the big Christmas Eve extravaganza before they got swamped the rest of the day. Hopefully he'd have time to sneak in some shopping, too. He still hadn't decided what to get Allie for her Christmas gift, and time was ticking away faster than he wanted to admit.

"Not physically full. Emotionally. I had an argument with my mom last night." She picked her fork back up and poked at her grits, now congealing on her plate. "I feel like there's a giant rock in my stomach."

"What happened?" Jordan pushed aside his computer to give Allie his full attention. Hope burst inside him that she might actually confide in him and take their working relationship to a higher level—one approaching renewed friendship.

And, if the tremor in his stomach every time he peered into her big blue eyes was any indication, maybe eventually something more.

"It's nothing. Forget it." But the sadness on her face stated otherwise.

"Allie, talk to me. You obviously need to vent."

She hesitated.

"You used to tell me everything." Regret sprawled across the table between them, and a distinct heaviness settled in Jordan's heart. "We used to talk for hours on the phone."

Sadness came into Allie's eyes, and she straightened. She shoved her plate away. "We'd better get busy. Where's that spreadsheet of figures?"

Jordan slowly opened his laptop, wondering how on earth his size-eleven loafer managed to fit inside his mouth.

Allie had two hours, a checkbook with a little bit of money actually inside and an entire store teeming with decorations, holiday music and people—yet she'd never felt less like Christmas shopping in all her life.

She bobbed her head in time to the familiar carol ringing through the gift shop but to no avail. Greta's Gifts had always been one of her favorite places to shop, but Allie was sorely lacking in Christmas spirit.

"Need some help, honey?"

Allie looked up as Greta smiled at her from across the counter. The older woman rang up a customer's purchase and slipped it inside a plastic bag. "You've been staring at that piggy bank for five solid minutes."

Allie sheepishly put the polka-dotted pig back on the shelf. "Sorry, Greta. I just have a lot on my mind."

"Holiday secrets?" Greta handed the customer his change and wished him a Merry Christmas before turning back to Allie. "I love shopping. Good thing I get a discount here." She tilted her gray head back and let out a generous laugh. "What do you think of my window display?"

Allie made her way to the front of the store to join Greta by the window. "It's beautiful." She studied the pink-and-green gift boxes, all tied with yellow bows. Sparkly fuchsia trees stood on each side of a stuffed polar bear, who sat proudly in a pile of glittery cotton snow. A large, carved wooden sign had *Merry Christmas* in yellow block letters above an arrangement of pink stockings.

"I wanted to branch out from the traditional red and green this year." Greta placed her hands on her slim hips. "I think there is something just so cheerful about pink and yellow."

"I agree." Allie couldn't help but smile at the excited store owner. "Well, I'm not a judge for the store-window contest, but if I were, you'd have my vote. It's very creative." In fact, Molly might like that porcelain figurine of pastries under a glass serving dish. It'd be a cute tribute to her new catering business—and a goodwill gesture toward their developing friendship.

"You're a doll." Greta took Allie's arm and tugged her over to the cash register. "And for that sincere little compliment, I have a gift for you."

Allie flushed. "Greta, that's not necessary."

"Nonsense. I see how hard you and Mr. Walker have been working on this festival for our town. Everyone deserves a treat now and then." She handed Allie a paper bag filled with a variety of candies from her display case. "You share them with that sweet Mr. Walker, now, you hear?" She winked.

Allie took the bag and thanked her. But she'd rather have handed the candy back than sit in front of Jordan again today and pretend that nothing was wrong. How dare he bring up their past at the diner like it was no big deal, like they'd amicably parted ways ten years ago?

Like her heart didn't still sting with the memory of losing her first love?

Allie made small talk with Greta as the older lady rang up the pastry figurine for Molly, promising the shop owner yet again that she'd share her chocolate with "that sweet Mr. Walker."

Wishing Greta good luck with the contest, Allie wrapped her scarf around her neck and headed outside. She didn't know what was more exhausting—trying to keep her heart out of Jordan's reach or trying to convince herself he didn't already have it.

She'd see him at the window contest tonight and then tomorrow at the big Christmas Eve finale. After that, who knew? Her job was only guaranteed through Christmas. At this point, it was safe to assume she hadn't acquired the loan she requested in Kansas City. It was time to move on with Plan B, which meant staying in Ginger Falls and finding work elsewhere. It'd be hard enough to handle living in the same town and bumping into Jordan periodically but impossible to work with him long term. Not with her traitorous heart whispering memories she tried to forget. Memories of warm hugs and late nights on the porch swing, laughing until they cried.

Memories she once thought she'd cherish forever.

Allie stepped onto the cold of Main Street and lifted her chin in determination. Regardless of where she lived or worked, one thing was certain. She and Jordan Walker were done making memories.

And the sooner her heart realized that, the better.

Chapter Ten

"I still think Theo's doughnut tree in the diner window should have won." Molly licked fudge off her thumb and offered the candy bowl to Allie.

Allie plucked a piece off the snowman platter before setting it on their mother's coffee table. "It was pretty cute. But Greta's window was adorable. I'm glad she got first place."

"So was Sophie. She had so much fun tonight that she fell asleep in the car on the way home. I'm glad Mom agreed to let us stay over so she could keep sleeping, especially with Tim having to work late." Molly adjusted the throw pillow in her lap as she nibbled on her chocolate. "Can you believe tomorrow is Christmas Eve? It seems each year the holiday flies faster and faster. Especially once you have children." She stopped short with a wince. "Sorry."

"It's okay." Allie finished her chocolate and wiped her hands on the snowflake-printed napkin. "I know you and Mom mean well. Having kids is a pretty big part of your lives." She stared wistfully at her parent's Christmas tree in the corner. "I'll experience that one day, hopefully."

"So, the big career girl wants the whole picture after all." Molly leaned back against the couch and groaned, one hand against her stomach. "Don't let me eat any more fudge."

Allie nudged the plate away from her sister as she pondered her response. "You could say that coming home has resurrected some dreams."

"Or Jordan has." Molly held the pillow up in defense at Allie's glare. "Oh, come on. Don't deny it. You guys still have a thing for each other."

"Attraction isn't the point."

"Neither is denial." Molly's eyebrow quirked.

"I admit I still have feelings for him. Seeing him after all this time just confirmed those feelings never completely went away. But I doubt he feels the same." Allie sighed. "Which just makes staying here in Ginger Falls all the more complicated."

"How so?"

Allie stared at her sister, as if the answer should be obvious. "I can't work for him when he's interested only in the professional. I'll make a fool of myself. He broke up with me once—and he's just trying to be a friend now. Probably feels guilty for the way things ended ten years ago."

"I wouldn't be so sure Jordan doesn't have feelings

for you, too. I think you're just blind to them because he broke your heart once—and you're too focused on your big dreams to see that a different kind of dream has landed right in front of you." Molly stood and headed toward the kitchen. "Want some hot chocolate?" She called over her shoulder.

"No," Allie muttered, as Molly's words rolled around in her mind. It was easy for her sister to say. She had a husband, a family, a career—all the pieces to the puzzle. And while Allie no longer begrudged Molly's happiness, it didn't make her words any easier to swallow.

Or was that because they were true?

"Hey, your cell phone was vibrating on the counter in here." Molly appeared in the doorway and tossed the cell to her. Allie caught it and checked the display. One new voice mail, from earlier that afternoon. She quickly pushed the password code to hear the message.

"Ms. James, this is Wilson Kennedy at the Kansas City Community Bank. I apologize for not getting back with you sooner on the status of your loan proposal." He cleared his throat, and Allie's suddenly sweaty palm gripped the cell tighter. Her heart hammered in her throat. Did they call about rejections?

The husky voice droned on. "I'm pleased to report your loan request has been approved. Please stop in our office after the holidays, and we'll go through the final paperwork then. Merry Christmas."

The recording ended with an abrupt click, and Allie's hand slid to her lap, absently hitting End to disconnect. She had the loan. Her own store. Her dream.

Then her stomach twisted into a tight knot, and she closed her eyes, her head dropping back against the couch.

But was it the right dream?

Jordan fumbled in his jacket pocket for his car keys. His cold fingers didn't want to cooperate, and he dropped the key ring twice before managing to hit the unlock button. The dome light clicked on inside the SUV, breaking up the darkness of Main Street. He slung his briefcase into the passenger seat and loosened his scarf.

He cranked the ignition, letting his gaze rest on the deserted town square. The store window contest had been a huge success. Tourists and locals alike had gathered to vote, and the first, second and third-place winners had all received plaques to hang in their windows. Hopefully that would drum up more business—and get the rest of the contestants fired up to enter next year. If Jordan had anything to say about it, the Gingerbread Festival would never again be a thing of the past.

His cell rang, and he flipped it open as he adjusted the heater vents. "Hello?"

"Jordan, it's Allie."

His heart jerked, and he quickly put his foot on the brake. "Allie, hi. Is everything okay? You left the contest pretty quickly tonight."

"I'm fine, I just…we need to talk." Her hesitant tone sent a tremor of nerves down Jordan's spine.

"Sure. What's going on?" He turned the radio low and slipped out of his gloves, settling in for the duration.

"I didn't want to throw you off guard tomorrow at work." Allie waited a beat. "My business loan came through in Kansas City."

"It did?" Jordan heard the crack in his voice, and he cleared his throat. "That's…great. Right?"

"Right." Allie's tone turned slightly guarded. "The call came tonight during the festival, and well, I thought you should be the first to know." She laughed, but it carried little humor. "I guess this is my official notice."

"I guess so." Jordan's stomach churned. "Well, congratulations."

"Thanks."

Silence hovered over the line, and then they both started talking at once.

"Ladies first." Jordan's free hand clenched the steering wheel in an effort to keep the tension out of his voice. Allie was leaving. Soon he'd have no more excuses to see her daily, to enjoy her laugh, to appreciate the way that blue scarf lit up her eyes.

Her voice filled his ear. "I was just saying we

knew my job here was only temporary. So it's not a problem, is it?"

"No problem at all." He rested his forehead against the cool leather of the wheel. It was only temporary—the job and, apparently, their relationship. "When do you leave?"

"The banker said I could come by next week and start talking details."

Next week? Jordan closed his eyes and gritted his teeth. "Things are happening fast, aren't they?"

"Seems that way."

Was that disappointment he heard in her voice?

"So, I guess I'll see you at the office in the morning. Then the big finale tomorrow night." Allie's tone lightened, and Jordan slumped against the seat. How pathetic was he, hoping she would be disappointed in her own choice?

"See you tomorrow. And congratulations again." He swallowed the thick lump in his throat. "You deserve this."

"Thanks, Jordan." Her soft words melted his defenses. "Good night."

"Goodbye, Allie." He closed his phone but made no move to drive away. He shouldn't be so surprised. He'd known the loan was a possibility since Allie's first day on the job. He had to admit that a part of him hoped the economy would force Allie to stick around town—and him—longer. But the bigger part that truly cared for Allie wanted her to succeed and live her dreams.

With or without him.

With a heavy heart, Jordan shifted the car into drive and pulled away from the curb. All around him tonight, people had teemed with holiday cheer, but now his spirits drooped like a child finding coal in his stocking. Ironic how ten years ago he'd unintentionally made Allie's Christmas the worst one she'd ever had.

Apparently this year, it was his turn.

Allie's stomach tightened as she stared at her bedroom ceiling. Molly and her parents had long since gone to sleep, but Jordan's words circled in Allie's head, keeping her awake—or rather, what he hadn't said. Was he not affected by her moving back to Kansas City at all? Their phone conversation further disproved Molly's theory that Jordan still had feelings for Allie. Sure, he'd probably miss her as an employee; after all, they had worked well together the past several weeks. But as something more? Not likely. She was fortunate to be leaving before she made a fool of herself for assuming otherwise.

Allie rolled over, pounding her pillow with one hand, pushing the fluffy feathers into place. She closed her eyes, but all she could see was the gazebo. Were all her relationships destined to end the same way—broken, scarred reminders of the past?

Despite the bad memories, she'd started to fall in love with the town again these past few weeks, investing her time and energy into helping give it a second chance. She could relate—after all, this loan was giving her the same opportunity in Kansas City. One more shot at making something of herself. One more chance to show herself—and her parents—what she could do. She'd be foolish not to take it.

But at what cost? If she moved, she'd be leaving behind the remains of her relationship with her family and abandoning the fledgling friendship she'd started with Molly—and Jordan. Though how much longer could she ignore her feelings for Jordan? No, it was best to leave, start fresh again somewhere that her past and present didn't mingle at every turn, where memories didn't linger on every street corner. Somewhere that didn't remind her of how her life could have been. Somewhere that she could forget Jordan once and for all.

Because Ginger Falls had nothing to offer Allie but heartbreak.

Chapter Eleven

Jordan's time with Allie was almost up. Today was Christmas Eve, and he still had no gift for her—nothing suitable to express his feelings, anyway. Cashmere scarves, fuzzy slippers and fruit baskets just didn't seem to say what he needed to tell her—and he was losing opportunities fast. After the big event that evening, Allie would spend the remaining holiday with her family and then head back to Kansas City to start her business.

And she'd be great at it. Jordan flipped through the work journal Allie had created, charting their progress through the Gingerbread Festival. The event had brought in more revenue than he could have hoped for. Ginger Falls was slowly earning its place back on the map, and after tonight, who knew how far word would spread? The local news promised to be on the scene at 8:00 p.m. sharp for the picture, and once Allie finished the town's new Web site, they'd be well on their way.

Mayor Cubley and the rest of the town committee

were ecstatic. At every event, they praised Jordan for a job well done, but he openly protested that the majority of the credit should be given to Allie. She'd worked so hard behind the scenes, keeping Jordan and his lack of organizational skills in line, handling the money they earned through donations and making sure deposits were made on time each day. Not to mention she always had a smile and an encouraging word for shop owners and tourists in town. Jordan wouldn't have been nearly as successful at his goal without her. They'd made a great team.

Too bad she couldn't see that.

The office door opened, and Allie breezed through, her dark curls dancing around her cheeks and the collar of her purple blouse. "Good morning."

"'Morning." He wouldn't lie. There wasn't much good about it—at least not in his heart at the moment. Jordan forced a smile, wishing he could permanently stamp Allie's appearance today in his brain. She must be more excited about her pending move than he'd first thought, due to the pretty flush in her face and the way she fumbled with her scarf before unwinding it from her neck.

"Busy day! What should I do first?" She draped her jacket over the back of the chair and sat, fingers twitching in her lap.

Jordan rubbed his temples briefly, trying to focus. "Um, I guess, first, we should…" He blanked.

"Call the media to confirm their attendance tonight?"

He nodded, eyes averted. "Sure."

"And then double-check with the pilot and photographer to make sure they're ready?"

He looked up. "Uh, yeah, that'd be great."

Allie pulled out her cell and started punching buttons, probably accessing her personal notebook she'd grown so fond of using these last few weeks. "Then I'll make sure our Web site is up and running so we can post the picture immediately after it's taken."

"Allie, what am I going to do without you?" The words slipped out before Jordan could catch them, and he sucked in a sharp breath as her expression tightened.

Allie's fingers froze, and she stared at the phone in her lap, her lips pressing together into a tight line as she tried to steady her breathing. "You said it wouldn't be a problem."

"But it is." Jordan stood and moved to the chair beside Allie, leaning forward and resting his elbows on his knees. "We're good together, Allie. You and me."

Was he talking about work or something more? Her chest constricted, and she clenched her phone with white knuckles, simultaneously wishing he'd go back to his side of the desk and stay beside her forever. "You know I have plans in Kansas City."

Jordan nodded, his gaze lowering to linger on her lips. "I know." His eyes asked a question she couldn't answer, and her breathing turned shallow. *Don't be stupid, Allie. Don't go there.* But the memories of their first kiss rushed toward her until their heady presence filled the room and drowned all voices of reason.

Suddenly all Allie could smell was the spicy scent of Jordan's cologne, the tangy haze of bonfire smoke and freshly burned leaves. She swallowed the lump in her throat. She could still hear Jordan's laugh as he tugged her to him that night at the senior party, feel his leather jacket under her palms, the sensation of his smooth-shaven chin and his lips against hers.

Tears of regret burned her eyes, and Allie blinked rapidly to clear them.

"I never apologized to you, did I?" His tone softened, and he gently picked up her hand. "I hated the way things ended between us, Allie. You deserved better than that."

She couldn't speak, couldn't think, just stared at his finger tracing the lines in her palm. "Then why?"

He ran a light touch across her knuckles, then folded her fingers against his. The warm pressure of his hand soothed her nerves. "I came back for you that night. But you were gone."

She searched his eyes for answers. "What do you mean?"

Jordan stood and pulled her up with him. "I tried

to find you, to explain what I had wanted to say before we started arguing. But then I saw you leaving with your dad and thought it best to stay away."

Allie risked a glance into Jordan's melted chocolate gaze, and her throat tightened. He'd come back for her, even after their fight. She swallowed hard. "What had you wanted to explain?"

"What I thought you already knew." Jordan ran a finger down the curve of her jaw, sending shivers down her spine. She kept her eyes trained on the top button of his dress shirt. If she looked at his lips again…

"That I was a kid, and you'd stolen my heart. It scared me. That I was torn between my feelings for you and needing to please my parents. My future was set up for me, Allie, a long time ago." Jordan sighed. "And it never included you."

The words landed a blow to Allie's rising hopes, and her body tensed. She quickly stepped out of his loose embrace and reached for her jacket, pain knotting in her throat. "I just remembered I need to check with Theo on some food preparations for tonight. I better hurry before his lunch crowd arrives." She blindly thrust her arms into the sleeves of her coat and headed for the door.

"Allie, wait." Jordan's voice pleaded across the office, but she was already heading toward the elevator.

She was through waiting on Jordan Walker.

* * *

The crowd tonight was thicker than ever before, both figuratively and literally. The temperature had dropped and heavy clouds formed above Leonard Mitchell's pasture, blanketing the stars in gray and causing everyone to have dressed in bulky layers for warmth. Even the local news crew shivered beside their van as they prepared their equipment for recording. Jordan flexed his fingers inside his gloves. It was cold but not nearly as frigid as the sadness that came with every thought of Allie's imminent departure from Ginger Falls.

And from him.

He tried to shove thoughts of Allie out of his mind, but his eyes found her like a magnet regardless of how much physical space he put between them. She stood at a card table set up by the gated barbed wire fence, arranging boxes full of flashlights, her dark hair grazing her shoulders as she worked.

Mayor Cubley appeared at his side and clapped Jordan's shoulder, a movement he barely felt beneath the layers of sweaters beneath his jacket. "Should we get everyone lined up? It seems like a good crowd has arrived."

Jordan squinted at his watch and nodded. "The pilot is on schedule to circle by at eight o'clock sharp for the picture. Everyone needs to report to Allie to pick up their flashlight and get into place. We staked the outline in the pasture yesterday for everyone to know where to stand. "

"I'll make the announcement." Mayor Cubley rubbed his gloved hands together in a brisk movement. "Goodness, but it's cold. I'm sure everyone will be glad to get back to Theo's Diner for cider and hot chocolate after this. Do you still want me to read the Christmas story?"

"Yes, at nine o'clock, in front of the gazebo."

"Will do." The mayor started to leave, then paused and studied Jordan. "You know, son, your coming back to Ginger Falls was the best Christmas gift this town could have had. I don't know where we'd be right now without you."

"I appreciate that, Mayor, but I didn't do much." Jordan looked around the crowd of children and adults, then anxiously back at the news crew. "Guess we'll see after tonight how well it all worked."

"Nonsense." Mayor Cubley's gray mustache twitched. "Regardless of tonight, you've already brought in revenue, donated your own money and secured leases on vacant properties—not to mention inspired the entire community to give this town another chance. Just look at this turnout! People are starting to care again, Jordan. That's not an easy task to accomplish."

"Thank you, sir." Warmth settled in Jordan's heart. He couldn't have done any of it without Allie, though.

The reminder of her partnership swept a cold wind across his spirit.

"You tell Ms. James I mean that toward her, as well." As if reading Jordan's mind, the mayor gestured to the card table of flashlights. "You two are quite the team. I wish there was something we could do to show our appreciation."

Allie and he *were*—a team. But not for much longer. Jordan swallowed against the pain. "This is my home, sir. I'm happy to do my part."

They shook hands, and the mayor moved toward the tables, clapping his hands for attention and issuing orders in his friendly, booming voice. Jordan's gaze instinctively went to Allie. He should tell the news crew they were almost ready, but his booted feet felt frozen to the ground beneath him, weighted by the heaviness of his heart. A line formed in front of Allie, and she quickly went to work handing out flashlights. Greta, the gift-shop owner, stepped up to the front and said something that made Allie laugh and gesture animatedly with one hand. Greta patted Allie's arm with a wide smile before leaving the line and heading toward the pasture.

A knot formed in Jordan's stomach. Allie had found her way back to town after years of absence, just like he had. Could she really leave it all behind for the second time in her life? With a sigh, Jordan shoved his hands in his pockets and strode across the frosty ground to the news van. He had the feeling she was just as eager, if not more so, to leave *him* behind.

And he couldn't blame her one bit.

Allie clicked her flashlight, the bulb covered in a purple plastic film, on and off as she made her way through the crowd to the stakes that marked the giant gingerbread man's top button. The cold breeze tickled her neck under her jacket and brushed tendrils of hair across her cheeks. She shivered. Yet despite the cold all around her, locals and tourists jostled for places beside the wooden markers, an excited murmur riding their wake as they craned their heads to the sky. The plane was due to come any minute. The news crew had their cameras set up across the pasture, and already a reporter was interviewing a family of four. From the looks of it, this event—like all the others—would be a hit.

The sense of accomplishment mingled with a suddenly overwhelming feeling of dejection. Allie drew a deep breath. She was making the right decision. Even though it was nice being back in Ginger Falls, her dreams and future lay within Kansas City. There was nothing for her here anymore.

A flash of red caught her eye, and she realized one of the flashlights was out of place. She stooped over to level herself with the child holding the light. "Whoops. Red is for the gingerbread man's mouth, little guy."

The boy's face puckered beneath his knit cap, and he pouted up at his mother. "I don't want to be the lips. Lips are for girls!"

"Trade ya!" A girl with long blond braids stepped to one side and held out her flashlight. "I'm green."

"What's green for?" The boy squinted with suspicion at Allie.

She tried to hide her smile. "The eyes."

The boy snatched the flashlight from the girl's hand and relayed his own before running to his new position a few yards away.

Allie shrugged at the boy's mother, who shook her head with a laugh. "Boys will be boys."

"What'd we do this time?" Jordan stepped up beside Allie with a smile. "I hear some gender-bashing going on."

Allie struggled to keep a straight face even as her stomach reacted to Jordan's proximity. *Oh, Lord, not now. I'm so close to leaving this all behind. Can you please tell my heart to wait a little longer?* She'd successfully avoided Jordan so far this evening, even if she couldn't help watching him interact with the townspeople and Mayor Cubley.

"Nothing at all." The woman kept one eye on her son, who was now staring at the sky with the others beside him. "My Kenny just wanted a more masculine piece of the gingerbread man."

"Let me guess. He was originally assigned the mouth?"

The woman laughed as she adjusted the collar of her jacket. "How'd you guess?"

"Boys will be boys, right?" Jordan mimicked her answer with a grin and then held out his hand. "Jordan Walker. Allie and I work for Ginger Falls, and we're glad you came out tonight."

She shook his hand. "Stephanie Haynes. It's nice to meet you—and we're happy to come. It's all Kenny talked about since seeing the ad in the newspaper. We're from a little town outside of Norton."

Allie regained her smile. "Well, we hope Kenny has fun. Don't forget to come back to Main Street after this event. We're having free carriage rides and refreshments in the town square." She glanced at her watch. "Yikes, it's almost eight o'clock."

"Time for the plane." Jordan cupped his hands around his mouth. "Places, everyone! Flashlights on and pointed to the sky!"

Allie quickly stepped into place, joy and dismay mixing as one as Jordan took the staked spot next to her inside the button. He clicked his flashlight on and aimed it toward the clouds. She turned and followed suit, telling herself there was no way she could feel his warmth from a foot away. But every nerve in her body remained alert to his presence, and she swallowed. *He doesn't want you, Allie. He said so himself this morning in the office. Don't make a fool of yourself.*

The crowd fell into an expectant silence as they

waited. A sudden whirring from the heavens broke the stillness of the evening, and a cheer spread throughout the pasture as the small red and white plane broke through the clouds. All around Allie, flashlights were held high and steady, sending a multicolored glow into the night. Tears of fatigue, joy and accomplishment pricked Allie's eyes, and she couldn't help but glance over her shoulder at Jordan. He winked at her and mouthed the words, "We did it."

She smiled back, despite the warnings in her heart, and nodded. "We did it."

Chapter Twelve

Allie held Sophie up to pet the nose of the furry white horse while Molly climbed into the empty carriage waiting by the curb on Main Street. Her sister shivered as she settled into the red leather seat. "I wish Tim were here tonight to keep us warm!" She held her arms out for Sophie, and Allie helped her niece climb into the carriage. "But I shouldn't complain. At least he's off work tomorrow for Christmas."

"That's what's important." Allie handed over a thermos of hot chocolate she'd brought from Theo's across the street. "Here you go. Be careful. It's hot."

"Thanks." Molly patted Sophie's leg. "Scoot over for Aunt Allie."

"I can catch another one." Allie helped drape a blanket around Sophie's lap, tucking her in against the cold.

"Don't be silly. There's plenty of room. Come on."

"Okay, if you're sure." Allie gripped the side of the carriage and started to hoist herself up. A familiar deep voice resounded beside her, and her hand slipped from the rung. Strong hands held her steady as she fumbled for a hold.

"Excuse me, ladies. Only two people per carriage."

She turned, Jordan's arm still bracing her weight on the carriage step. "What do you mean? Sophie hardly counts as a person."

"Hey!" Sophie's eyebrows furrowed together in indignant protest.

Molly tried and failed to stifle her laugh behind her glove. "You know what Aunt Allie means. You're smaller than an adult."

"I have an empty carriage waiting just ahead." Jordan's dark gaze met Allie's. "We can finish up some business details."

"All right." Allie climbed off the step with reluctance. A few more hours in Jordan's presence, then she would be done. After tonight, she was officially through with her job and could spend the rest of her time in Ginger Falls at her parents' house, drowning her sorrows in cocoa and sugar cookies. But shouldn't she be more excited about the prospect of starting her own business next week?

Allie followed Jordan to the next carriage, waving at Sophie as their buggy took off down the street. Jordan offered a hand to help Allie board, but she waved it off, awkwardly maneuvering her way onto the seat alone. She pressed against the far side as Jordan climbed in beside her.

"Comfortable?"

With his leg inches from hers and his warm peppermint-scented breath even closer? Not really. "A little cold, but fine."

"Here." Jordan grabbed a blanket that had been stowed under the seats of the carriages and opened it for her. She tucked the green fabric around her legs, grateful for the extra padding between her and Jordan.

"Better?"

"Yes, thanks."

The driver slapped the reins against the horse's back, and their white steed began prancing his way down Main Street. Allie couldn't help but relax as fresh flakes fell from the sky, dusting the town like powdered sugar. Snow clung to her curls, and she brushed at them with her mittens. Just as her dad advised years ago, she shouldn't let a man interfere with her favorite holiday. She smiled as tiny crystals tickled her nose.

"You have snow in your eyelashes." Jordan pulled one glove off and ran his finger gently across her eyelid. His touch was even lighter and more feathery than the snow. Allie's shoulders tensed, and she pulled away, immediately missing the warmth of his hand as he slowly let it fall back to his lap.

She tried to focus on her surroundings, instead of the unsteady thumping of her heart. All around them, locals and tourists alike enjoyed the festival. Several kids stood in the street, trying to catch snowflakes on their tongues while their parents laughed and talked nearby, rehashing the gingerbread man adventure from the hour before. Main Street hadn't been given a true makeover yet with the funds they'd earned, but the warmth and light of the people participating made the city brighter. Jordan might have raised the town's awareness of its critical condition, but he did more than that—he made them care. Ginger Falls was going to be just fine.

But was she?

"You're quiet." Jordan rested one arm behind Allie on the back of the carriage. He didn't touch her, but she felt the heat like a hundred radiators in the dead of winter. "I thought you'd be happy after our success earlier. The news station promised they'd have our story on the ten o'clock news tonight and again in the morning."

"I am happy. Just thinking. It's been a long couple weeks." She gestured to the camaraderie around them as the driver made a turn around the square. "But worthwhile."

"The mayor paid us a high compliment tonight. He's very proud of all we've done. I told him it wasn't much, but he insisted we made a big difference."

"I know don't about 'we,' but you did." Allie

flicked at the snow gathering on the blanket in her lap. "You deserve the praise. I was actually just thinking the same thing."

"You were?" Jordan's head tilted with surprise.

Allie let out a long breath, the warm air clouding the frigid night. "Jordan, just because we have a bad past behind us doesn't mean I can't notice your good qualities."

"So I do have them?" His tone joked, but his eyes were serious.

Allie touched his arm before she could think better of the action. "Yes. You always have. If you were a jerk, it'd have been easier to get over you all those years ago." The memory of his earlier words in the office shadowed her mind, and she pulled away. "Although what you said this morning helped a little."

He frowned. "What are you talking about?"

"You informed me that your life's plan never included me." The pain struck fresh, and Allie turned her head, focusing on the swish of the horses' tail. "Which is fine—it just would have been nice to know that before we dated our senior year." She'd spent enough time missing someone who obviously didn't miss her, and she wasn't eager to keep the cycle going.

Though lately, her heart's cry insisted she didn't have a choice.

"Allie, you left the office today before I could

finish what I was saying." Jordan took her hand. She tugged it back, but he held on. "My *parents'* plan never included you—I said nothing about my own."

Her hand stilled under his. Jordan hoped the sudden lack of struggle proved she was listening— and melting that icy, defensive wall around her heart. He tightened his grip on her hand, feeling the warmth even through their gloves. "That's what I was trying to tell you that night. I was a frustrated kid, feeling the pressure. I never meant to hurt you."

"Do you ever think about what might have been?" For the first time in what felt like ages, Allie looked directly into his eyes. The intensity of her gaze nearly made Jordan forget the question.

He eased away an inch to bring her face into focus. "All the time." He hesitated. "Did you…date much? In Kansas City, I mean."

Allie shrugged but didn't move her hand from his. "A little. Nothing serious." She looked away. "You?"

"The same." Jordan drew a deep breath, hoping he wouldn't regret the next words leaving his mouth. "No one was ever you, Allie." She smiled, but it held more bittersweet emotion than joy. He wished he could touch her lips, turn them into a real smile, a grin brought by mutual caring—instead of nostalgia.

"I can relate to that."

Jordan's heart jump-started at her quiet response, and hope dared to bloom, like a rogue winter flower fighting a blanket of snow. He squeezed her fingers beneath his. "Can we start over?" She hesitated, and Jordan filled the silence. "I know you're leaving next week, and it technically doesn't make a lot of sense to start a long-distance relationship, but I'd do whatever it takes to make it work this time."

The carriage turned again, lapping them around the center of the square, and Allie's gaze landed on the gazebo. "That's the thing, Jordan. It wouldn't work." Her voice turned wistful. "We're like the gazebo."

He followed her stare to the worn structure on Main Street. "How so?"

"The gazebo was once this beautiful icon of Ginger Falls. And look at it now. It's practically falling apart. It's tired of even trying to hold together, Jordan." She drew a deep breath. "And so am I."

Jordan couldn't find the words to argue as the carriage pulled to a stop by the curb, and Allie quickly climbed out the other side.

They'd come full circle.

Jordan sat on the edge of the broken gazebo bench, watching the sound crew roll and carry the cords used for the Bible reading. The tourist crowd had dispersed an hour before, leaving nothing behind but a few pieces of trash blowing beside the cans on the curb and the potent scent of horses lingering in the air.

Tired of trying to hold together. Allie's words pierced his mind. He knew the feeling. He was tired of trying to pretend that Allie didn't still claim his heart, didn't still take his breath away every time she brushed her hair out of her face or smiled at him across the room. He still loved her—without a doubt and possibly even more now than he did as a teenager. Because now he knew what was at stake. He knew what it felt like to live without her.

But to Allie, their relationship was like the bench he sat on and the entire gazebo—worn, crumbled, stained. Jordan pressed his fingers against his temples as he cast a look around their once-special spot, practically flooded with memories. What Allie didn't realize was that all the gazebo's problems were on the surface. The foundation was still secure. It just needed a little work and a lot of loving attention.

Could he and Allie have the same second chance?

An idea began to fill his mind—slowly at first, like the snow falling outside the gazebo's open walls and then faster, bringing more details and sustenance. He stood and checked the braces supporting the gazebo's roof, gave the rail a solid shake, then stomped one booted foot hard on the floor. It offered a sturdy echo, and he smiled as the mayor's words looped through his head. *I wish there was some way we could show our appreciation.* It'd take a few phone calls, more than a few favors and maybe even a bit of a Christmas miracle, but it would work. It had to. Jordan had finally found Allie's perfect Christmas gift.

Her mom's spiced apple cider didn't taste nearly as good as Allie remembered—probably because of the bitterness that seemed to fill her from the inside out. Sitting cross-legged on the floor by the lit tree, Allie dejectedly set the teacup back on its saucer.

"Does it need more cinnamon?" Her mother asked from her perch on the couch.

"No, Mom. The cider is fine." Allie sighed as she stared up into the twinkling array of lights and ornaments, unable to fully appreciate the beautiful sight or the soft strains of Christmas music drifting from the stereo in the corner. "It's just me. I haven't been able to find my usual Christmas spirit this year." At least she'd been able to finish buying her family's gifts. They nestled under the lowest branches of the trees, waiting for the next morning when Molly, Tim and Sophie would arrive for lunch.

A lump knotted in her throat at the thought of her sister and niece. How many moments of Molly's and Sophie's lives would she miss by moving away? Starting a new business was risky stuff. It would require her full attention—she'd have very little, if any, time to visit Ginger Falls.

Allie shook her head at the irony. A month ago, that fact would have been a perfect excuse to avoid seeing her family. But now that her relationship with Molly was on the mend, the arrangement brought more depression than relief.

Her mother set her cider on the coffee table as her father brought a platter of cookies into the living room. "What's this about no Christmas spirit?" His voice boomed as he settled onto the couch by Allie's mom, reminding Allie of the years he played Santa for her and Molly growing up.

She hugged her pajama-clad legs up to her chest. "It's been a rough year."

"No harder than some." Her mother bit into a bell-shaped cookie. "What's really going on, Allie? I thought you'd be excited about your loan being approved and the prospect of starting your own store."

"I was." Allie shook her head quickly. "I *am*." She sighed. "I'm just a little mixed up." She felt more jumbled inside than the tangle of lights her parents had spent three hours unraveling for the tree. *God, I need clear direction. You've practically handed me all my dreams on a silver platter—so why doesn't it bring joy?*

Her father sipped from his steaming mug of coffee and then pierced her with his familiar, knowing gaze.

"Maybe your lack of excitement means this isn't the right path."

Panic stirred her stomach. "But it has to be."

Her mother frowned. "Why, honey?"

Allie swallowed and looked away, fighting back a wave of emotion years in the making. "I have nothing else. I'm not good at anything else." The truth of her statement wrapped her in a prickly blanket, and she shuddered.

"That's not true." Her father shook his head. "You're a smart woman, Allie. You've made some choices in the past and are living the consequences, but that doesn't mean they were wrong choices. They've brought you where you are today."

"And where I am?" Allie gestured around the gaily decorated living room. "Unemployed, single, living off my parents." Tears pricked her eyes. "I'm a failure."

Silence filled the room.

"Just admit it." Allie sniffed. "I know you've thought that the past few years after I turned down the consulting position."

"We've never once thought that." Her mom moved from the couch to the floor beside Allie. "I see now that I've made some comments about yours and Molly's differences over the years that hurt you. But we've never considered you less worthwhile or successful than your sister."

"She's right," her father said. "You alone see

yourself as a failure. We see you as brave. You've taken risky roads before, and that requires courage. You're about to head off down another one with your new store, and I have complete confidence that you'll get it right."

"As do I." Mom wrapped one arm around Allie's shoulder. "And if you need help, ask. Molly knows a few things about starting a business. She struggled at the beginning, too. No one is perfect."

Perfect. Allie wiped her eyes with the back of her hand as she sent her parents an appreciative smile. Had that been her subconscious lofty goal that landed her in this mess in the first place? Had she tried too hard or put too much pressure on herself? Maybe she'd allowed her former boss's words to cut a little too deeply. Maybe Allie could have done more, but life happened. Sales dropped. Shops closed.

Hearts broke.

I'd do whatever it took to make it work this time. Jordan's words flashed back in her head, bringing with them equal parts joy and sadness. Joy because she'd always imagined this happening and sadness because he was too late. Her dreams were finally within reach, and she'd be a fool to miss her chance and risk her heart on Jordan. What if she gave up everything for him and he hurt her again?

She thought of the way she'd let her professional life influence her personal life and grimaced. She might be brave in some aspects, but in regards to her heart, she'd been overly protective. Maybe Jordan deserved a second chance after all.

Maybe she did, too.

"Thanks, you guys." Allie hugged her mother and then stood and bent over the couch to hug her dad. "You've given me a lot to think about."

"We should have had this talk a long time ago." Her father patted her back as she straightened. "I hope we helped."

"More than you know." A hint of Christmas spirit began to seep inside Allie. "I'd better head to bed. Santa comes tonight, you know." She winked at her parents as she headed toward the stairs, feeling lighter than she had in months. Tomorrow, she'd talk to Jordan. What was stopping her from giving him another chance, other than the fear of taking a risk?

Chapter Thirteen

Christmas morning dawned clear and crisp, covering the earth with a thin white blanket of snow. Allie sat on the floor by the tree in her favorite plaid pajamas amid piles of discarded wrapping paper. A plate of sausage balls were nestled in her lap—another of her favorite traditions. She felt like a kid again, and this time, the thought brought warmth rather than feelings of failure. She popped another sausage ball in her mouth and laughed at her father, who tried tossing a wad of torn paper into the trash bag across the room.

The doorbell rang, and her dad missed his shot, the paper bouncing off the side of the plastic and nearly hitting the tree. "Interference!"

"Who could that possibly be this early?" Allie's mom stood and peered behind the lacy living room curtain at the front porch. "It's not even eight o'clock."

Dad stepped over his new pair of suede slippers and the box containing the tie Allie just given him and joined his wife at the window. "Maybe it's our neighbors with cranberry pie. They brought one last year, remember?"

Mom shook her head with a smile and moved away from the curtain. "Actually, Allie, I think it's for you."

"Me?" Allie stood, clutching the knotted belt of her new pink robe. "What do you mean?" She rushed to join her parents at the window, tissue paper crunching under her bare feet, and looked outside.

Jordan.

Her breath caught. She didn't want to see him, not with the tumult of last night's emotions still churning. Her hope for any relationship with Jordan had dissolved into a thick puddle of reality. She was moving in mere days, and his place was here, in Ginger Falls, reconstructing the town into what he imagined—into what it deserved. Once again, their life goals were taking them in opposite directions, but this time, she was the one leaving.

"Run and get dressed. I'll let him in." Her mother stepped toward the front door, apparently taking Allie's stunned silence as agreement.

Allie hurried up the stairs away from the Merry Christmas greetings echoing around the foyer. Jordan's warm, familiar voice floated up the stairway with her, and she shut the bedroom door against it.

She dressed quickly in jeans and a blue sweater, pausing to dab on a hint of makeup. Even if this conversation was just going to cause inevitable tears and heartache, at least she'd give Jordan a good memory of her face to carry with him until he moved on.

She knew she'd be doing the same.

The foyer was quiet, and she hesitated at the foot of the steps. Was he still here? After the way she and Jordan parted ways last night, she wouldn't have been surprised if he hadn't wanted to say goodbye before she left next week. He'd expressed his heart in the carriage, and she'd shot him down. That had to hurt.

In fact, she knew it hurt. He'd done the same to her ten years ago to the day.

"Jordan is outside." Allie's mother crossed the foyer into the kitchen, carrying their empty breakfast dishes from the living room. "I told him you'd be right there. Molly and Tim won't be here for a few hours, so take your time visiting."

Allie drew a steadying breath. "Thanks, Mom." She slowly opened the front door and stepped onto the porch. The cold winter air pricked her lungs. She wrapped her arms around herself for warmth.

Jordan sat on one of the rocking chairs, gently gliding back and forth. He planted both feet on the porch when he saw her, abruptly stopping the motion. "Merry Christmas."

"Merry Christmas." Allie stood by the door, not moving toward him, unable to trust herself in his presence. After realizing how she truly felt last night, the pain of their imminent separation would be that much harder if she allowed herself to enjoy his nearness. She kept her arms crossed, guarding her heart.

Jordan walked toward her, eyes bleary and tired, shoulders slumped. "I came to give you your Christmas present."

"What?" Shock reeled Allie backward a half step. "Jordan, you shouldn't have. After what I said last night—"

"Shh." He pressed one finger against her lips, and Allie stilled under his touch. The pleading in his gaze nearly broke her heart. "Just come with me. Please?"

How could she say no when he looked so exhausted? What had he been doing? She looked back into his eyes and then averted her gaze. "Let me grab my coat."

She was coming. Relief overcame the exhaustion he felt from staying up all night, and a brief rush of energy filled Jordan's limbs. He'd wondered the entire time he worked on Allie's present if she'd even allow him the chance to give it. He mentally rehearsed the words he wanted to say, but his tired brain could offer nothing witty or convincing. He'd have to wing it. *God, I could use some backup here.* He sent the plea into the heavens. But no matter what happened this morning, at least he knew he tried his hardest to show his heart to Allie.

The rest was up to her.

"I'm ready." She stepped back on the porch, sliding her arms into the sleeves of her jacket. They descended the steps and climbed into Jordan's SUV.

Jordan fastened his seat belt, hating the awkward silence between them. He cleared his throat as he started the engine. "Looks like we got a white Christmas."

Allie smiled and nodded as she buckled her belt but didn't speak. Jordan jerked the car into Reverse and drove as quickly as the snow and speed limit would allow. He didn't blame her for the quiet, wouldn't know what to think himself if the roles were reversed. Any other man would declare him crazy for expressing his feelings again, less than twenty-four hours after being shot down the first time, but he had to give it all he had. The only thing more painful than losing Allie for the second time in his life would be losing her without having done his best to win her back and living with that regret for another ten years.

He slowed the car as they approached the town square. Main Street was deserted, as most people were tucked contentedly in their homes, sharing Christmas with their families—though a good portion of them were probably as exhausted as he.

Jordan parked and got out. Allie frowned through

the window as he approached her side. He opened the door and she unbuckled. "Jordan, what's going on?"

He stepped aside as she slid out. "We're here."

"My present is Main Street?" Doubt crinkled her eyebrows, and she worked her lower lip between her teeth.

"No." He gently took her shoulders and turned her north.

Her gaze landed on the giant green tent where the gazebo normally stood. "Where's the gazebo?" She frowned, confusion shadowing her face. "I don't understand."

Jordan led her to the edge of the tent and lifted the giant flap. She peered inside and then sucked in a sharp breath. Jordan's pulse pounded in his temples, and his heart stammered against his chest as he tried to decipher her glazed expression. She turned to him, eyes wide, and he said the only thing that came to mind.

"Merry Christmas, Allie."

The gazebo stood proudly under the tent in front of Allie, like a groom dressed in his finest attire. She pressed her hands to her cheeks to contain her shock. The once faded and worn paint now glistened as white as the freshly fallen snow outside, and the crumbled bench had been replaced with a new wooden one, complete with black iron scroll-work. A beautiful lantern chandelier hung from the ceiling, draped in garland and berries. The entire roof glowed softly with tiny Christmas lights, illuminating the soft shadows under the tent.

Allie turned to Jordan. "This is for me?" Her hands shook, and he took one of her gloved palms in his.

"All for you. Come see up close." He led her up the stairs onto the platform. "Watch out for the space heaters."

She carefully stepped over one of the large heaters by the stairs and spun a slow circle on the deck, soaking in the details. Tears filled her eyes, and she blinked rapidly to hold them back. He'd done this for her. Even after the way she'd blown him off last night, he'd sacrificed time, money and sleep. He'd taken an even bigger risk than she had—he was risking his heart.

"How did you do this?" She stared up at the twinkling lights above, imagining how long it must have taken Jordan to complete this enormous task.

"I'd brought some sample pieces of my design business with me when I moved here, like the chandelier, and kept them in storage." He grinned, temporarily erasing the lines of exhaustion around his eyes. "And I had a little help from the townspeople. Turns out they're all pretty grateful for our work in Ginger Falls these past few weeks."

She shook her head. "This is amazing. I can't believe it."

"The snow almost ruined the entire plan, but Mayor Cubley had this tent in the city's storage center and let me use it. Theo and Greta and a lot of the other townspeople helped paint and pound nails and offered space heaters to help the paint dry in the cold. I sent everyone home around 2:00 a.m., but I stayed up all night." Jordan glanced around the structure, his eyes lingering on various spots as if appreciating the work for the first time. "I didn't know how else to show you how I feel."

Allie's heart jump-started, and she turned her gaze fully on the man in front of her. "What do you mean?"

Jordan tugged her toward him, and warmth flooded her veins. Her cheeks flushed, but she didn't pull away.

"You said our relationship was like this gazebo, worn and tired. Well…" Jordan's voice trailed off as he reached and tucked a curl of hair behind her ear. "I wanted to prove otherwise. The gazebo was able to be restored to its former glory and then some. I have the same faith that with a little work our love can do the same."

The tears she'd worked so hard to keep at bay crested and slipped down her cheeks. She looked away from his intense gaze. "This is awful. You— and the entire town—gave me this amazing gift, and I didn't get you anything."

"Having you walk back into Ginger Falls and into

my life was the best Christmas present I could ever have hoped for." Jordan wiped her tears away with his thumb and cradled her face in his hands. "Allie, you're the one for me. I've never been able to get over you, and you know what? I don't want to try anymore."

She closed her eyes, absorbing his touch, soaking in the sincerity of his words like a tree receiving a much-needed rain. Could this work? Could she risk her heart? She met his gaze with her own, hoping he could see her heart reflected inside. "I feel the same way."

His eyes darkened with emotion, and he slid his hand from her cheeks to the nape of her neck, drawing her closer. "Marry me." He whispered against her lips. "I don't have a ring yet, but you've had my heart for longer than I can remember. Marry me, and make this the best Christmas I've ever had."

Allie teetered at the crossroads of faith and security. She had to decide—extend her heart, or keep it tucked away out of reach. But she was tired of living in fear, tired of playing it safe. She wanted to feel. She wanted to love and be loved.

She wanted to take risks.

Allie quickly closed the distance between them, sealing their hearts and her answer with a kiss. He wrapped his arms around her, and she slid hers around his neck, clinging to the familiar warmth of his touch. How could she have ever thought she belonged anywhere but by Jordan's side?

He slowly pulled away and rested his forehead against hers, grinning. "Was that a yes?"

"Yes." She kissed him again for good measure and then broke apart, breathless.

"Allie…I know how important your goal of opening a business is for you. I could never stand in the way of your dreams." He nodded, as if confirming his internal struggle. "I'll go with you to Kansas City. I owe you that much and more."

She shook her head. "Jordan, no. Your place is here. Ginger Falls needs you. This is your passion."

"Then what do we do?"

"I'll stay."

Jordan opened his mouth to protest, but Allie gently touched his cheek to quiet him. "I'm serious. I don't want to be away from you or my family. I want to be a full-time aunt to Sophie, and now that my sister and I are on better terms, I'd like to be more involved in their lives. This is how it was meant to be." She hesitated. "Maybe I could try to open a store here eventually."

Jordan wrapped his arms around Allie's waist and smiled down at her. "You know, there is a prime spot on Main Street just begging to be leased. Think your odds are good of acquiring a business loan here instead?" He winked.

Allie couldn't help the grin that spread across her

cheeks. She could have her dream and at the same time, help her hometown that she'd fallen in love with once again.

Thanks to the man she'd fallen in love with once again.

"Oh, I'd say they're pretty good." She curled her fingers into the collar of Jordan's jacket. "Especially if I have a certain boss's referral on my application."

"That can definitely be arranged." Jordan's smile faded as his gaze turned serious.

"I love you."

"I love you, too." She nestled against his chest, amazed at how she still fit perfectly beneath his chin. Some things never changed, and today, she'd never been more grateful for the fact.

"There's just one more thing." Jordan let go of her long enough to point above them.

Allie eased back and craned her head to look up. A tiny cluster of mistletoe dangled from the bottom of the chandelier. She smiled into Jordan's eyes. "I think that, too, can be arranged."

He leaned in and pressed his lips against hers. "Merry Christmas, Allie."

She kissed him back with her entire heart, joy filling her spirit to overflowing. "Merry Christmas, Jordan."

* * * * *

Dear Reader,

With Christmas comes many traditions, and I was excited to give Allie the opportunity to share the joy of my favorite—lying under the Christmas tree and peering up through the shiny, twinkling branches. Like Allie, I started doing that as a child and have no idea why, other than it seemed as if for those few treasured moments I was transported to another world.

Years ago, Someone *was* transported to another world. Jesus came from heaven to become the best Christmas gift we could have ever hoped for—life. Because of His sacrifice, we have hope, joy and peace—all the things that make up the warmest feelings of Christmas.

This year, as you embrace the holiday season with your family and enjoy your own traditions of food, fun and fellowship, take time to remember a special Baby born in a manger on a cold winter's night. Accept the free gift of salvation that Jesus offers us today—it won't fit under the tree, but it'll fit in your heart for eternity.

Merry Christmas!

Betsy St. Amant

QUESTIONS FOR DISCUSSION

1. When Allie first arrived back in Ginger Falls, she carried a negative assumption of herself and saw failure in everything she did. How did this negativity affect the way she thought others saw her?

2. How would you feel if you ran into an ex love you'd never fully gotten over, without warning? What would you say?

3. Jordan was passionate about his hometown. How did his enthusiasm to restore Ginger Falls affect the entire community?

4. Does your hometown host an annual event everyone looks forward to like the Gingerbread Festival? If you could start an event in your city, what would you choose to do?

5. Jordan and Allie carried a lot of baggage from their past, along with several misunderstandings. Do you think if Jordan and Allie had been more open in their conversation at the gazebo all those years ago, things could have turned out differently?

6. Jordan was afraid of staying in a relationship with Allie because of pressure from his family to do bigger and better things. Have you ever sacrificed a relationship or friendship at someone else's prompting? What was the result of such a decision?

7. The gazebo held both good and bad memories for Allie, though definitely better after the story is over. Is there a specific landmark you associate with a memory in your life?

8. Allie's favorite holiday tradition was lying under the tree and staring up through the lights into what was called "Christmas." What special traditions do you and your family enjoy every year?

LARGER-PRINT BOOKS!

GET 2 FREE LARGER-PRINT NOVELS PLUS 2 FREE MYSTERY GIFTS

Love Inspired®

Larger-print novels are now available...

Love Inspired®
SUSPENSE
RIVETING INSPIRATIONAL ROMANCE

Watch for our new series of
edge-of-your-seat suspense novels.
These contemporary tales
of intrigue and romance
feature Christian characters
facing challenges to their faith...
and their lives!

NOW AVAILABLE IN REGULAR
& LARGER-PRINT FORMATS

Steeple
Hill®

Visit:
www.SteepleHill.com